I0645751

STEVIE-GIRL AND THE PHANTOM PILOT

THE PHANTOM SERIES ~ BOOK ONE

ANN SWANN

5 PRINCE PUBLISHING

STEVIE-GIRL AND THE PHANTOM PILOT

ANN SWANN

The Phantom Series
Book One

5 PRINCE PUBLISHING & BOOKS, LLC

PO Box 16507, Denver, CO 80216

www.5PrinceBooks.com

Digital:ISBN-10:1-63112-205-3, ISBN-13:978-1-63112-204-0

Print:ISBN-10:1-63112-205-3, ISBN-13:978-1-63112-205-7

STEVIE-GIRL AND THE PHANTOM PILOT, Ann Swann

Copyright ANN SWANN 2017

Published by 5 Prince Publishing

Cover Credit: Viola Estrella

Third Edition 2017

This book is dedicated to my handsome husband
who has always believed in ghosts and in me.

PROLOGUE

It was the late 60s. The Beatles had washed across America like a British tsunami, Vietnam was a grainy, green and black dose of unreality on the evening news, a bunch of hippies had taken over San Francisco, and there was a heck of a rainstorm pouring down on Woodstock. But I didn't know all that then.

I was a little bit lost, looking for something. I swear I didn't go looking for a ghost...well, okay, maybe I did. But I didn't expect to find one. Heck, I was just a kid. I didn't expect much of anything.

1
_____

I was twelve years old, standing knock-kneed in pigtails and ripped denim in front of a haunted house, trying to dig up enough courage to go inside. But I was terrified. I'd read the books and I'd seen the movies on Shock Theater. No matter what, you don't go inside the spooky old house. No matter who dares you, no matter what lures you. You do not go in.

Hand trembling, I opened the door.

The warped wood screeched when I pushed it. I expected that. But I didn't expect the dusty floorboards to moan with my every step. I tried not to think about it. I was in. I'd lived around the corner from this house all my life and today I'd finally garnered enough willpower to walk inside.

The light was dim, murky with dust motes and cobwebs. The curtains were little more than yellowed rags hanging in tatters. The windows themselves were so filthy the light coming through was leached of its goodness by layers of grime.

I'd been in the grocery store buying a loaf of bread for supper. The store was only a block from our house. They knew me there almost as well as they knew my Gramps. On my way to the check out, I saw old Mr. Pearcy in the frozen food section, reading labels. *Probably trying to figure out which one might taste the most like his wife's cooking.* It had been only a couple of weeks since I'd seen Mrs. Pearcy's obituary in the newspaper.

I read the newspaper almost every morning over breakfast. I loved reading of any kind. As a joke, Gramps once wrapped my new cereal box in duct tape so I couldn't read it at the kitchen table. I could tell you the nutrition information for almost every kid's cereal known to mankind. Reading's just my thing. It always has been.

"Get the smothered steak," I whispered as I walked by Mr. Pearcy. "It's yummy." I hurried on and got in line to pay for my bread.

"Thanks, Stevie-girl," I heard him reply.

When I glanced back over my shoulder, I saw that he'd stuck his head back inside the stand-up freezer. The open door facing me had fogged over, but I could make out his silhouette. As I watched, he backed out and held the flat rectangular box in front of his face so that I could see it. He'd replaced the turkey and dressing with the steak. I raised my hand to give him a thumbs-up as he lowered the box into his shopping basket.

All the breath suddenly drained from my body. Mr. Pearcy was gone. On top of his plaid shoulders sat an oozing skull. Wisps of thin gray hair clung to the patchy flesh.

I closed my eyes and sucked in air. When I looked again, it was just Mr. Pearcy standing there with his hand raised, looking at me as if I'd slipped a cog.

"You okay, honey?" The voice came from the woman next to me in line. "You look awfully pale." She laid her hand on my shoulder as if to steady me. It was obvious she hadn't seen anything unusual except for me pale and shaking.

"I—I'm okay," I replied. "Dizzy for a second." I smiled my best white-liar's smile. "Just got over an inner ear infection."

She nodded the sympathetic nod of a grandmother.

I paid and hurried toward home keeping a sharp eye out for Mr. Pearcy, but I didn't see him again. *Must've been my imagination. Or a trick of the light. Maybe it was just a reflection off the frosty door.*

Now, looking at the steep, dark staircase in front of me, I inhaled slowly, feeling my lungs expand all the way down, moving my diaphragm just like Mr. Morrow, the music teacher, said we should. The image of Mr. Pearcy's raggedy skull kept trying to creep into my mind, but I wouldn't let it.

"Lalalalala," I sang under my breath. Singing always calmed me down and made me feel better. Besides, I knew I hadn't *really* seen anything. Stopping here on the way home had been in the back of my mind ever since Gramps had asked me to run down to the store. Just the *idea* of going in the haunted house was probably the reason I'd seen that awful thing. Over-active imagination, that's what Gramps always said.

I started forward again. The house was deserted. No one had lived here for *ages*, and that made it spooky, as if it were holding in a breath, waiting for something. But what if someone else *was* here? Someone, or *something*, living upstairs where no one could see? A bum, or a bandit hiding out from the law? I knew it was possible because my Gramps was a semi-retired cop. He said the worst monsters were not under the bed or in the bedroom closet. Instead, they walked among us. I believed him. Gramps was all I had left. I had to believe him. Guess that's why I didn't really put much stock in things like ghosts. I was too smart for that, too worldly. But man, was it spooky!

Whaaaa. The floor cried like a baby as I put my foot down a little too solidly. I jerked it back up to balance on one leg like a blue-jean clad flamingo. Carefully, I lowered my foot and inched backwards toward the door. That was enough. I'd proved to myself that I was brave. Besides, the landing at the top of the stairs was wreathed in shadows and even the creepy light from the windows was fading fast. Thinking of bums and bad guys had convinced me I shouldn't be there.

Dark streaks wafted across the room. *That's nothing but the shadows of trees outside the window, swaying in the breeze. That's all.* I might not believe in ghosts and monsters, but I did believe in intuition, that feeling that tells you when it's time to book, and right now, my intuition was strong. It took all my will power not to turn and run, but I wanted to prove to myself that I could do this without panicking, so I held my breath and continued creeping backwards, afraid to take my eyes off that stairway. That's when I heard it—a *sliding* sound. Like shoes across a sandy floor.

That was it. That was my undoing. My willpower was all used up. I twisted around to run and crashed right into a tall figure in a soft blue shirt.

"Boo!"

I shrieked and began pummeling the figure with my loaf of bread.

"Hold up!" The figure laughed. "You're killing me!"

"Jase!" I shoved both my hands against his chest and ducked under his arm. The plastic bread sack slithered from my grasp. "What are *you* doing here?" My breath was raspy. I was furious with him for laughing. And for scaring me.

Easily fending off the attack, Jase caught the bread before it hit the floor. His thick blond hair fell over one eye as he handed it back to me. "What am *I* doing? What are *you* doing?" He looked around the dilapidated manor.

I puffed out my chest, prepared to tell him it was none of his business, but we'd stirred up a cloud of dust. I began to sneeze instead.

"Are you—are you—*Ahhh-choo!*"

"Gesundheit! Am I what?"

Dashing outside, I sneezed again and again until I was

finally able to take in a few breaths of fresh air. "Are you following me?"

Jase leapt off the porch. He was tall—the tallest boy in our class.

I made it a point to walk down the steps. The yard was weedy in some places, bare dirt in others. It was getting on toward five o'clock, and the light had taken on that funny hue that meant sunset was not too far away. It reminded me that even the Indian summer was just about gone. The day had that orangey kind of feel to it, like autumn leaves.

Jase sat on a rusty iron bench that encircled the base of the oak tree shading the front yard. The tree and the deep pockets of shade it provided made the old house even creepier. "I wasn't really following you," he said. "I saw you come out of the Piggly Wiggly, and I was just going to catch up to you to see what you were doing."

Still standing, I propped my feet, first one and then the other, on the bench beside him so I could retie the laces on my red Converse high-tops. I wasn't sure what to say. We weren't friends, just classmates.

Jase leaned back against the tree trunk. "I saw you come in here." He looked up at me, but I could tell the slanting rays of the sun kept him from really seeing me. He shaded his eyes with one hand. "Do you come here a lot?"

That made *me* laugh. "Yeah, all the time. Didn't you see the brave way I raced up the steps and charged right inside?"

He laughed a real laugh, not a making-fun laugh. "Yeah, I did see that."

Realizing how late it had gotten, I started toward the gate. "Gotta get what's left of my *weapon* home for supper." I held up my bedraggled loaf of bread. "My Gramps is probably wondering what happened to me."

Jase folded one long leg up and caught the edge of the bench with his own sneakered heel. I noticed he wore some kind of track shoes. He laced his fingers together around his knee. He looked comfortable, as if he might just sit there all night with the sunlight and shadows playing chase across his friendly face. But he didn't. As soon as I started through the gate, he stood up.

"Guess I'll see ya in school tomorrow."

"Yeah." He smiled. "See ya." Then he walked back up on the porch and pulled the creaky door shut with a bang. In our haste to get out, we'd left it standing wide open. I thought that was something, brave or stupid, I wasn't sure which. I was pretty certain I couldn't have made myself go back up there and close the door. Something, a hand or an arm or a claw, might reach out and grab me.

I let my gaze travel toward the upstairs window. A shadow twitched the edge of the ragged curtain before melting away into the gloom.

Jase shivered, shrugging his shoulders as if wishing for a jacket. I didn't think he'd seen anything. He wasn't looking up like I was. Had he felt something? He turned and hurried out the gate, but I was already halfway down the sidewalk. I glanced back just as he flipped his hair off his forehead and cut north across the open yards. After a few steps, he began to jog.

I was home in two minutes. My house was close to everything in Crossroads, our small Texas town. The school was four blocks north, the store a block south, and the police station where my Gramps was now the daytime dispatcher was just a few blocks south and east. One block west is where my ex-best-friend, Karla, used to live. But at the end of school last year, Karla's dad joined the Marines because he lost his job and the military was taking every able bodied man they could find. So this year he was in Vietnam and Karla was in California living with her mom and grandparents.

I tried not to walk west if I could help it. It made me really sad to pass Karla's house with someone else living there. Besides, the old Taylor Mansion was the other direction, sort of behind the Piggly Wiggly, and that's the reason I went there, because the last time I'd heard from Karla, she said her dad hadn't written in a long time. They were really worried about him. I thought if I could make myself go into the haunted house —something Karla and I had often dared each other to do but had never actually worked up the nerve for—it would give me something to put in my next letter. Something to make her feel better, take her mind off her dad.

Truth-be-told, I thought maybe if I was brave enough to do that, it would somehow help Karla's dad to be brave. Sometimes, I wished my own dad had gone to Vietnam. At least then my Mama wouldn't have been looking for him, and maybe then she wouldn't have had the wreck that killed her. *Oh, I shouldn't have thought that. I take it back, I take it back, I take it back! I wouldn't wish Vietnam on anyone, please and thank you and cross my heart and hope to die.* I made an X over my heart, closed my eyes and kissed my thumb.

It was the only thing I could think of to undo my horrible thought. Vietnam was a *bad* place. I really wouldn't wish it on anyone, not even my sorry excuse for a father. He'd left one evening after receiving a phone call from parts unknown, and then he'd pulled the old disappearing act.

"And I didn't even know he was a magician!" Gramps said after we'd landed on his doorstep in the middle of the night a couple of months later, broke and evicted 'cause Mama didn't have enough rent money.

I learned all about the war in Vietnam from watching the six o'clock news, the soldiers in green and black camouflage crossing muddy rivers with their rifles held high above their heads. Sometimes they would have jungle leaves and vines stuck on their helmets. Gramps said that was camouflage. I was pretty sure that someday we would see Karla's dad on there, crossing a river. He was one of the oldest guys in his outfit. He would be easy to spot.

Gramps took the bread and wrapped a few slices in foil to heat. It didn't *have* to be heated. It just made us both feel better if the bread was warm, as if Gran was still here to bake it herself. But she'd died from a stroke about three years ago and we both missed her terribly. We told each other we heated the bread because it stayed soft and the butter melted better, but I knew the truth. I'm sure Gramps did, too.

He held up the plastic bag. The bottom was full of crumbs. "What happened? Did'ja drop it on the way home?"

I shook my head. "Had to hit a boy with it." I popped a strand of spaghetti in my mouth to test for doneness.

"What'd he do to deserve a beatin' with our supper?"

I giggled. "Just startled me, that's all." I didn't want to admit I'd been in the old Taylor place. We'd never talked about it, but I was fairly certain it would be off limits if he knew.

"Keep 'em on their toes, kid," Gramps replied. "But, Stevie..."

I looked up because the tone of his voice had changed.

"You'd tell me if anyone was really causing you trouble, right?"

I laid my head against his shoulder. "You know I would, Gramps. I didn't mean to hit him with the bread. He didn't do anything but say boo."

Not quite convinced, Gramps said, "Okay, just let me know if anyone ever *does* need a beatin'. Deal?"

"Deal." I held out my hand so we could shake on it.

2

The next day in school, Jase looked up when I walked in. We'd always attended the same school. There was only one junior high school in our whole town, but this was the first year we'd ever been in the same class.

"Hey." He glanced up as I was walking past him to get to my seat in the back. I sat back there in hopes of being invisible.

"Hey." I'm such a social butterfly—small talk's my middle name...not.!

Until yesterday, the most we'd ever spoken to each other had been, "Pick me, pick me!" when one of us was in charge of choosing for teams during PE. Except for the other day when he'd been asked to pass back the graded Math tests. When he handed me my 98, he'd said: "Wow, you did good. I hate fractions." But then he'd moved on to the next person, and we hadn't spoken again.

Today, we were having a class discussion on the first half of the novel *My Side of the Mountain*. I *loved* the book. I'd read the whole thing as soon as it'd been assigned.

"What do you think, Stevie?" Mrs. Boyd asked. I gulped. I wasn't paying attention. Mrs. Boyd never did that. She never cold-called on someone whose hand wasn't even raised. That's what I liked about her. She didn't try to catch you out. Not usually, anyhow. Guess my luck had just run out.

"Sorry," I admitted. "I didn't hear the question."

Mrs. Boyd just smiled. "I said, why do you think the book was named *My Side of the Mountain?*"

I opened my mouth to answer. Such an easy question.

"Because he thinks he's the only one who lives there."

The voice had come from Jase. He hadn't raised his hand or anything.

The teacher frowned slightly. "That's correct, Jase. Was that true?" She looked at me expectantly.

"Not if you count the wildlife and Bando," Jase said.

I looked at Mrs. Boyd and shrugged as if to say: *Boys, what can you do?*

Mrs. Boyd gave up and closed her book. She turned to the board and wrote out a list of questions. "Take out pencil and paper and answer these questions in complete sentences." She looked over her half-moon glasses. "You have forty minutes to the bell. Place the papers on my desk before you leave."

Around me I heard groaning and mutters of "Pop quiz! Oh, man…" But I wasn't worried. I loved tests like this. It was sort of like discussing the book in writing. I looked at the first question. *Describe the setting.* Piece of cake, I thought, putting pencil to paper.

I was about three-quarters of the way through the test when I saw Jase stroll up and lay his paper on Mrs. Boyd's desk. He was the first one done.

I glanced at the clock. There was still plenty of time. What was with him today? Jumping on my answers like that. He'd never done that before. And now, being the first one through? I was usually the first one through.

Two spaces in front of me, he rummaged through his desk

until he found a library book, and then he slumped down in his seat and began to read.

I felt my pencil trying to speed up all by itself. I had to mentally stop and take charge. *No hurry, I thought. No hurry at all. Plenty of time.* I hated being second. Now my train of thought was all messed up.

Finally, I finished the last question and turned in my paper. Mrs. Boyd smiled and immediately began to check off the answers. I could see Jase's paper pushed off to the side with a big red 100 written at the top. The sight of it made my mouth clamp shut into a tight, thin line.

When I started back to my desk, he glanced up, and then quickly looked back down at his book. I passed by him and plopped into my seat just as the bell rang.

Groans erupted all around us.

"Complete the question on which you are currently working, then give me your paper," the teacher said. "And if you really need a few extra minutes, you may stay."

Furious scribbling all around.

I gathered my books and headed to the door. Jase was already gone.

Outside, the fall air was wonderful. I felt better already. I usually loved anything related to Literature class, but today, Jase had really thrown me off. Oh, well. It was Friday.

I took off running toward the bike rack. My green Stingray was right where I'd left it this morning. I flung my books and notebook into the wire basket, hooked the strap across them, unchained my lock, and then took off, running beside it just long enough to build up some speed before leaping onto the banana seat and pedaling like mad.

Jase was in the park, sitting on a picnic table.

I thought about riding right on by and ignoring him. But as I got closer, he held up his hand in a stop motion—so I slowed.

"Thought you'd be coming through here," he said.

I slammed my foot down on the pedal and my rear tire skidded around in a half-circle leaving a good-sized mark on the rough trail. "Why?" I couldn't keep the edge off my voice. I wasn't sure why he'd felt the need to show me up in class today, but I hadn't been impressed.

Jase looked down at the ground. "Just figured anyone with a cool bike like that would ride through here every chance she got." He stood up and started to walk away.

I felt bad. "Hey—" I had no idea what I was about to say. I just knew I didn't want him to walk away with his shoulders hunched up like that. "Why'd you answer all my questions?"

He stopped and turned around. "Thought I was helping you out."

"Helping me?"

He shifted the books under his arm. "Yeah, when you didn't answer right away, I thought you didn't know."

"Oh." Understanding rushed over me. "Nah...I was just daydreaming. Mrs. B. never calls on me. I just wasn't listening."

Jase nodded and rocked back and forth on the balls of his feet. "Sorry."

"S'okay." Now I really felt bad and stupid. "I mean, thanks."

He studied me for a moment. "You finish the book yet?"

I nodded. "You?"

"Yeah. I really liked it."

"Me, too." I pedaled toward him slowly. "What's your favorite part?"

Jase fell in step beside me. "The part where he trains Frightful."

"Oh, I loved that, too. But I think the best part was the Halloween party for the animals. It was exciting and sort of frightening."

"Give you nightmares?" Jase's arched his eyebrows as he asked the question.

"Nah." I laughed. "You?"

He shook his head, and pushed his hair off his forehead. "You think any kid's folks would really let them move off to the wilderness like that?"

I contemplated that for a while. "I guess my dad would. He took off on us when I was small, and as far as I know he's living in the wilderness. It's obvious he doesn't care where I am, so yeah. I guess it could happen." I waited for him to respond, but he stayed quiet. "What d'you think?" I finally asked.

"Yeah. I agree with you. I don't think mine would notice me missing either." He walked beside me as I rode slowly along the path that eventually came out just a couple blocks from my house.

"You got a bike?" I asked.

"Sure. Got a flat, though."

I nodded sagely. I knew all about flats, but I was lucky. Gramps always took mine down to the PD and someone there would air it up for me.

"If you get it fixed, we could ride downtown tomorrow." I looked at him carefully. "I'm going to the music store to see what new records they got in."

"Yeah?" He brightened up. "I got an album by Steppenwolf last week. You like that one?"

"I love *Magic Carpet Ride*. You like The Beatles?"

"Doesn't everyone? I'll bring my radio tomorrow. We can hook it on your basket."

I nodded again. The leaves rustled overhead. They were just beginning to change. Halloween would be soon, but for now the trees were holding on to their treasures. Only a few leaves trembled to the ground when the breeze kicked up. Not the evergreens though—the pines and firs, the cedars—they held their shape, and their damp, fragrant needles made the little park green and cozy. We neared the exit to my house. "You live this way?"

Jase shook his head. "Other side of town, north of the hospital. We have a few acres there."

For the first time, I noticed that his eyes were a clear cool green, like rainwater in a mossy stream. I didn't quite know what else to say. "I guess now you have to walk all the way back through the park?"

"No big deal." He shrugged. "I walk or ride my bike everywhere."

I glanced up at my street sign—North 6th Street. "So you wanna meet somewhere tomorrow?"

"How 'bout here? You get up early on Saturday?"

I shook my head. I didn't want to admit that I still got up and watched Saturday morning cartoons—*The Flintstones, The Jetsons,* even *The Monkees*—not actually a cartoon, but still my favorite show besides *American Bandstand.* I usually ate my bowl of *Alpha-Bits* cereal while wrapped in a blanket in front of the TV. For some reason I didn't want him to think of me as a kid, even though we were probably the same age.

"That's all right. The music store doesn't open till ten anyway."

I pedaled slowly home. My Gramps was due at any time. He got off work around four. I let myself in with the key that I kept on a string around my neck. The house was pleasant and familiar, but something felt off. I threw open the living room curtains to let the strong autumn light inside.

Something was still different. I dumped a heaping spoonful of Nestlé's *Quik* into a glass of cold milk and stirred and stirred, the spoon clanking musically against the sides of the heavy jelly-jar glass. As always, there were a few clumps of powder left when I was done, but I took a deep drink and smashed them against the roof of my mouth with my tongue. Small bursts of powdery chocolate exploded on my taste buds. From the cupboard, I took a couple of vanilla wafers.

Sitting at the kitchen table, I smoothed my hand across the cool Formica, trying to understand why I felt so odd. This was the exact same routine I went through every day after school—chocolate milk and vanilla wafers.

Maybe it was just him. Jason Lee—Jase. I'd known him forever, since first grade at least, so why was he so friendly all of a sudden? Not that I minded exactly. He was kind of cute. Joanie Lamp always had a crush on him. Said he gave her his ID bracelet last year. Wonder if that was true? Knowing her, she'd probably tricked him out of it.

I crossed the scarred linoleum floor and rinsed my glass in the sink. *Leave it to Beaver* was on TV. Normally I would be in there watching it. I always wished I had a big brother or sister, someone to look out for me like Wally watched out for the Beav, but that was never going to happen. I was standing there letting the water run over my hands, daydreaming, when I heard Gramps's key in the door.

For supper, after Gramps got cleaned up and relaxed a bit, we ate Spam sandwiches in front of the TV on the same old metal trays we always used. We liked sitting there so we could watch the news, but we still didn't see Karla's dad, just some helicopters lifting off amidst a hail of gunfire.

Gramps shook his head. He never talked about his own time in the service. I know he went to Germany in 1944. I just don't know what he did there. We read about WWII in History class. The teacher said lots of veterans wouldn't talk about it, especially if they got anywhere near those horrible death camps.

"I LIED to you about the nightmares," Jase said as soon as we met up the next day. He was on a tall blue bike. It was strictly no frills. The battered black seat was wound round with black electrician's tape where the stuffing was trying to escape through a gaping split. Beside him, pink tongue lolling, was a sleek black and tan German shepherd with moist amber eyes that looked like they belonged in a saint's face instead of a dog's. "Name's Lady," he said.

I leaned over and held out my hand, palm up, totally ignoring Jase. The dog immediately gave me an approving lick as I gently caressed her smooth triangular head.

I'd been up for hours already, hardly watched cartoons at all, and didn't even mind that I was missing *The Monkees*. Well, not too much anyhow. Gramps was working. Although he was a dispatcher, having taken the daytime desk job after we lost Gran, he still had to work weekends and holidays just like regular officers. He just didn't have to work overnight anymore. I suspect that was because of me, and I was glad. I was pretty sure I wasn't brave enough to stay alone overnight yet.

After milling around the house for awhile, I'd finally gobbled down a piece of toast, drank some juice, pulled on my jeans, tee-shirt, high-tops, grabbed my jacket from its hook beside the door, and took off.

The weather was early-morning cool, and damp from the overnight dew, but I knew from experience that the dew would burn off later when the sun got high enough.

I was sitting cross-legged on a table waiting for *him* this time. "Whaddya mean you lied?" I scooched over so he could sit beside me on top of the cold cement table. He chose to sit on the bench part near my feet instead. Lady claimed a spot of thick grass under a tall elm.

"I *do* have nightmares," he said. "A lot."

My eyes must have mirrored my confusion.

"It has to do with something that happened a while back."

"Over the summer?"

He shook his head. "Last winter," he said. "Here, read this story I wrote. Then you'll understand." He handed me a thin sheaf of notebook paper. I was surprised his handwriting was so legible.

THE SHEPHERD
By Jason Lee

THE WEST TEXAS night wind whispered and whistled around the window frames. I was in my mom's favorite chair reading *The Tell-Tale Heart* when I heard the stuttering drone of a small plane. In our rural setting, it sounded very low and very loud.

Then the noise stopped.

Lady, the German shepherd I'd found lying mangled and near death beside the road, was standing in front of the picture-window, head cocked to one side.

The silence was thick and cold.

As we watched, the tail of a small plane disappeared behind the line of firs west of the house. There was still no sound but the wind.

I dialed the operator and told her what I'd seen. She immediately patched me through to the Sheriff's office so I could tell the dispatcher what had happened. Then I ran outside to see what I could see. Lady was right behind me.

My dad's old ranch truck was in the driveway. Without thinking, I fumbled around for the flashlight in the glove box. Mom was at a ladies Bible-study group, and Dad was out of town, but I knew how to drive the truck. I've been driving the truck around the ranch since I was old enough to reach the pedals.

Lady jumped in and we started off. Following the quarter

mile driveway to the road, I looked at the fir trees for my point of reference. Lady began to whine.

I jumped out to open the big gate across the driveway, but the wind tore it from my grasp. The sound of iron pipe gate hitting iron pipe fence made a hollow *gong* like a church bell. Lady jumped out and I drove on through just in time to see her feathery tail disappear between two trees.

Then I saw the plane. It was a four-seater, white with blue lettering, and it was upside down, its propeller and three landing wheels undamaged. Apparently the pilot had been attempting to glide into the field when one of the wingtips touched down gouging a deep trench in the earth before flipping the little plane over on its top. On a still night, he might have made it.

I shined the flashlight all around.

"Hello!" I called. The wind hooted at me through the trees.

The cockpit was crumpled. I would have to crawl underneath the wing for a closer view. "Anyone in there?" I did *not* want to stick my head inside that darkness.

"Here." The voice came from behind me.

I spun around, dropping the flashlight. It rolled over and over in the dirt shooting light this way and that until I snagged it and aimed it at the voice. "Oh!"

A tall, silver-haired man stood beside Lady.

"Are you okay?" I stepped closer.

He was way too calm. He patted my dog absently.

"I think so," he replied.

I shivered, but it wasn't from the cold. "Is anyone else in the plane?"

"I'm not sure." His voice was flat. "Did you look?"

"Not yet, but I will." He's in shock, I thought. I ran back to the truck for something warm.

"Here." I held out a spare jacket, the only thing I could find.

"No, thanks," he said.

My heart thumped into the back of my throat.

"Please, come to the truck. This wind is *fierce*."

He rubbed Lady's head. "Not cold, are we, girl?" The dog was a statue. To my surprise, she actually seemed to be pressing against the man's leg.

I tried to smile. "Then we'll just stay right here until the ambulance comes." I moved the light away from his face. There was *something* about his eyes.

Taking a deep breath, I turned back toward the plane. I knew I had to check for other people. In the distance I could already hear the welcome wail of a siren.

"That's not necessary," the man said.

I wasn't sure if he was referring to the ambulance, or to my intent to stick my head into the cave-like cockpit.

"I was alone." His voice was a whisper. "We all are."

The wind kicked up as the words left his mouth. A gust caused Lady to shift her feet as the chill air ruffled her fur. The moonlight fell in slanted beams.

I had to say something to break that awful silence. "Sure you don't you want to sit in my dad's truck?"

He gazed down at Lady. "She knows I have to go." He smoothed her fur absently. "She's been there before."

I remembered the day I'd found her half-dead beside the road, the victim of a hit-and-run driver.

The man's gaze rose to my face. His eyes were the same color as his hair.

The siren was deafening. I looked over my shoulder thankful to see the pulsing strobes. "Here!" I waved my flashlight at the emergency vehicle.

I turned back to the pilot, but he was gone.

There was only Lady, trotting off across the field.

"Hey! Mister!" My tone was strident.

The ambulance attendants hurried toward me.

"I'm the one who called. But there was a man—" I turned a quick circle.

The paramedic simply bypassed me and crawled under the wing of the plane where he immediately shined his big flashlight onto the face of the silver-haired pilot. The man was still strapped into his seatbelt harness upside down in the dark cockpit.

The EMT had to yell to be heard over the wind. "Got a pulse?"

The paramedic shook his head.

I backed away.

Even from outside of the plane, I could hear the men sawing at the fabric of the heavy-duty seatbelt. There was a horrible thud as the body fell from its seat.

The wind had gained even more strength. It was all *muscle*. It bent the trees and rocked the truck as I climbed inside. Starting the engine, I spotted Lady in my headlights. She was growing smaller and smaller.

I put the gearshift into drive and eased my foot off the brake. I couldn't go home without my girl. I drove slowly forward, circling the crash site, hoping for another glimpse of her familiar, loopy gait.

Instead, what I saw was the sullen glint of moonlight on silver as she led him away, across the darkest shadows of the field.

The End

"YOU WROTE THIS?" Awe made my mouth hang open like a Venus flytrap.

Jase nodded and took the rumpled pages from my hand. "I

had to. I had to tell someone. So I put it in a story. I've written lots of stories. Only this one is different."

"Wow. I didn't know you could write like that. Does anyone else know you write fiction?"

"It's *not* fiction." His voice was quiet. If it had been a color, it would have been solid white.

"What do you mean?" My heart skipped a bit.

He looked away from me. "It happened. It really happened just like I wrote it."

I hopped off the table and went to stand in front of where he was looking. My jeans were damp from where I'd been sitting on the cement table. I got right in his line of sight. "It happened? The plane, the pilot, your dog, Lady?"

Jase nodded. "Just like I wrote it. Man, I've never been so scared in my life." He gulped, turned his face away, and wouldn't look at me at all. "Until the next night."

I just stood there, watching, waiting for the punch line. 'Cause I knew this wasn't real. It had to be a joke. *Ghosts were not real!*

Jase's voice, that white, flat voice, was almost inaudible. I had to lean over to hear what he was saying: "The next night it happened again."

I guess I was shaking my head without even knowing it. Must've been backing away, too. Suddenly, Jase was off the cement bench, walking down the path. He hadn't even taken his bike.

"Wait!" I ran to catch him.

He stopped, but didn't turn around. I thought I heard him snuffle as he swiped at his face with the sleeve of his flannel shirt. Lady raised her head a few inches off the ground and looked at us, but she didn't move. I got the feeling she was not a young dog.

I caught up to him and grabbed his sleeve, just above his

elbow, forcing him to look at me. "What happened the next night?"

Doubt and trust wrestled each other across his face. After a moment, trust won out. "The guy appeared in my bedroom."

I gasped and covered my mouth with my hand. I couldn't help it. I thought, *why is he saying this? This is not a good joke!* But his face looked crumpled, like an old brown paper sack. I decided maybe he wasn't joking. "You mean the pilot?"

"Same one. Same silver hair, same silver eyes." He was staring at me, trying to judge my reaction perhaps. He was a whole head taller than me. "I didn't believe it at first either."

"Why me?" I blurted. "Why tell me?"

That stopped him.

I hadn't meant to say that. It just popped out.

With a sigh, Jase led me back to the picnic table and we sat down. "Because you seemed so brave when I saw you walking up the path to the old Taylor place like you'd done it a hundred times before."

"I had—in my mind."

That brought out a brief grin. "That's why I followed you that day."

"So you *were* following me."

He held up his hand. "I was hoping you might help me. You know, figure out what's going on. I wrote the story to give to Mrs. Boyd, see what she'd say, but then I saw you."

I sat quietly for a moment. This was not what I expected when he asked me to meet him this morning. I did believe him, even though I didn't personally believe in ghosts and spirits and all that. It was obvious something was going on.

I had to tell him the truth. "First of all, I just went in the old house because of my best friend, Karla. We were always trying to get up our nerve to go in the old haunted house, and now that she's gone and her dad is in Vietnam, I just did it as a way of being brave for her or him or something." I could hear how stupid that reasoning sounded when I said it out loud.

"Karla Smith? She moved at the end of last year, didn't she?"

I nodded. Tears formed under my eyelids. But I wasn't going to cry. I rubbed my lids roughly. I hated to cry. No one ever saw Stevie Rae Sanders cry. Not even my Gramps. "I miss her." My words were ragged. "She was the best friend I ever had."

He nodded. My sniffling didn't seem to bother him. He didn't even try to get me to stop like most people do when they think they see tears.

"Did you see anything inside the house?"

Glad of the subject change, I smirked. "Nothing, but you."

He laughed lightly. "Touché. By the way, did your bread make it the rest of the way home?"

I hiccupped. "Yeah, we ate all the little pieces with lots and lots of butter." I was being silly and sarcastic, but I couldn't seem to help it. "And my Gramps wanted to know if he needed to add to the beatin' I gave you."

"Wha'd you tell him?" His voice was serious.

"Told him I'd let him know after today."

He didn't say anything, just stood up and walked to his bike. From his pocket he pulled a small, gray transistor radio and tuned it to our local station—KWES—they played *all the hits all the time*. Not surprisingly, the tune, *War*, was playing. It was one of the most popular songs of the day.

"Here." He laid the radio gently in my wire basket. I could tell by the way he handled it that it meant a lot to him.

"It's my brother's." He tapped the gray plastic with his forefinger. "He's in Vietnam, too."

My lungs felt crushed inside my chest. I couldn't even get enough air to speak. I had no idea his brother was there when I was rattling on and on about being brave for Karla's dad. Finally, I rasped, "I'm sorry. I didn't know."

"It's okay," he shrugged. "I'm sorry about your friend." He hooked my book strap across the radio so it wouldn't bounce out while we were riding. *Sugar, Sugar*, a song by the Archies, came on. It lightened the mood a little, and if Karla had been with me instead of Jase, I would've been singing along at the top of my lungs. I almost did anyway.

Lady waited until she was sure we were actually going this time before she glided along behind us like a soft-coated shadow.

3

The Crossroads Music Store was on the square. It was a deep, narrow building with a storefront of plate glass covered over with signs and posters. They not only sold records of all kinds, they also sold sheet music, and musical equipment like guitar strings and reeds for wind instruments like clarinets and saxophones.

Today, we were just interested in records. I rifled through the racks of 45 rpm singles while Jase thumbed through the albums. His brother had told him to look for one by Creedence Clearwater Revival. He said they were even better than the Beatles. I didn't say it, but I wondered how his brother knew so much about current music when he was way over there—thousands of miles away.

"I love this place," I said as we stepped back out of the coolness of the store and onto the sidewalk in the sunshine. Lady lay next to our bikes in the narrow strip of shade afforded by the store's awning.

The streets of our tiny town of Crossroads are red brick. They were laid when the town was incorporated back around the year 1900. All the main streets were the same. They formed a square around the courthouse, which was ringed with live oaks just like the old Taylor place—very shady.

Shops lined the square: everything from the City Drugstore where you could eat lunch while your prescription was being filled, to the Model Shop, the women and children's clothing store that Gramps said was too high-falutin' for us. We shopped at Anthony's Department Store where they sold clothes for the whole family. There was also a Sears and Roebuck Store where you could pick up the items you ordered from the catalog, and a Perry's Five and Dime where I usually spent my allowance if I couldn't find a new record to buy.

"So, you wanna come to my house and listen to some music? Maybe go out to the field where he crashed to see what you think?"

I'd almost forgotten why I was really here. "Well, okay. But, Jase?"

He stopped, one leg thrown over his bike, new album under his arm, Lady watchful and ready. "Yeah?"

"I'm not really brave. I think you might have the wrong person to help you." I didn't mean to sound whiney. Looking at the horizon, I don't know what I expected him to say. I turned on the radio to cover the silence. *Build Me up Buttercup* was playing —another of my favorites.

"C'mon." Jase took off on his bike and I followed. It was so different, riding along with this boy. I was used to hanging out with Karla, and sometimes one or two other girls, even Royce, the class clown. We'd been a group. We'd done things like a little school of fish, all at once, no individual stuff. But this, this one-on-one with a boy I hardly knew, this was something else again.

I assumed we were going to his house until he stopped at Dal Paso Drug Store. It wasn't the new, modern City Drugstore. It was across the square, on the good side, by the Model Shop. Dal Paso was on the opposite side, by Benny's Bail Bonds. It was ancient, and tall, at least three stories with dark brown brick and an apartment with open windows on the upper floor. In front, it had thick double wooden doors set into the corner like the entrance to the pearly gates—if the gates were deep lustrous brown.

Even the Palace Theater down the street didn't have an entrance like the Dal Paso. The Palace did have all those fantastic murals though. The western scenes featured cowboys lassoing steers amidst saguaro cacti with a desert sun setting behind them. Great entertainment before the movie even started. Classic stuff.

But so was the Dal Paso.

Jase hopped off his bike and leaned it against the lamppost. That lamppost made me want to cry. It reminded me of the one time my dad was here for Christmas, before he disappeared into the Twilight Zone. I was just a little girl, maybe seven. He was drunk, but not sloppy, just happy, and we came to town to shop for Mom. It was Christmas Eve and the square was jam-packed with shoppers.

The lampposts were decorated with garlands of greenery and bows, and the stores were all lit up and merry with spray-on snow and dancing battery-operated elves. If I let it, my memory would insert some real snow here, but this is West Texas, and that would probably be pushing it. I do know the courthouse speakers were blasting Christmas carols and I think someone must've been serving eggnog because it seemed like every man over the age of twenty-one was way too jolly.

We were outside Barton's Furniture Store when Dad saw some old buddy and stopped to shoot the breeze. Maybe they were discussing something private or just for grown-ups because all of a sudden he jabbed twenty bucks in my hand and said, "Go on in there and find something for your Mom."

I must've looked confused.

"Look for a vase or a lamp or something," he said, jerking his thumb toward the furniture store.

So I did. I found the most horrific gold-colored Chinese vase with a red dragon painted on it. I had just enough money. Of course, at the time I didn't think it was horrific, I thought it was sublime, but when we got home it was too big to gift wrap so Gran helped me tie a ribbon on it and we hid it behind the tree.

I didn't know it would be the last Christmas present I ever got her. It was also the last time I saw my dad. Something important came up. He got a call, and he never looked back—just took off. At least that's how it seemed to me. Then one day Mama got word he was in Amarillo, so she took off to find him. But on the way, her car was hit by a semi truck. She never made it past Lubbock.

Jase held the door open for me, and I held the transistor out to him. He smiled and slipped it into his shirt pocket just like he'd done at The Music Store. "Want a Coke?" he asked.

I nodded. It felt so strange being in here with Jase. This was where teenagers came when they were *dating*. He ordered our Cokes and joked around with the guy behind the counter as he accepted a paper cup full of water for Lady who was guarding our bikes.

He smiled at me, took the water out to Lady, then came in and sat down in one of the red vinyl booths. I was still looking at the revolving rack of comics by the front door. I'd been here before, but now, it's like I was seeing it all new.

The floor was dark, smooth wood. It matched the exact hue of the immense wooden blades of the fans circling lazily overhead. The counter where the druggist worked was taller than me, and the six booths sat off to one side like a series of afterthoughts.

I finally put the Richie Rich comic back into the rack and strolled over to the booth. Jase had bought our drinks and was watching me but trying to pretend he wasn't. I sat down across from him. "Thanks for the Coke."

"Thanks for coming to help me," he replied. But of course, I hadn't done anything yet. In fact, I was really growing worried about the whole situation by this time. I knew my Gramps would pitch a fit if he suspected even half of what was going on.

"What 45 did you buy?" He'd been paying for his album while I was still looking through the singles.

"*Crimson and Clover*...I left it in my basket!"

"It'll be okay." He grinned and held up his thin paper sack from The Music Store. "I put it in here with mine." Slurping the last of his drink, he looked up at me expectantly. I was finished too. I didn't want to drink too much and have to go to the bathroom. That would be mortifying.

We stood up to leave. "I need to check in with my Gramps," I said. "It's getting close to noon and he'll wonder where I am." I hesitated with my foot on my bike pedal. "Jase..."

He looked at me.

"Did you tell your parents about the guy?" The sun was almost directly overhead. I wanted him to say no. Then I could say, well, you need to, and I'd be released. But he only looked away, stared at the courthouse square.

"My dad said quit being a sissy—there's no such thing as ghosts. Mom just walked away like she didn't understand what I was saying. She does that a lot now that Rusty is over there, in 'Nam."

He didn't give me a chance to reply. He just turned north, headed toward my street. The square, like everything, was only a few blocks from my house. But before we got to my street, we had to pass the old Taylor house.

In the broad noon light, it looked more sad than scary. "Wanna go in again?" he asked.

His red flannel shirt looked warm, its colors were sharp

against the light. Being Saturday, there were several people out working in their yards raking leaves and washing cars.

"Hey, Mr. Pearcy!" I was relieved to see the older man. I didn't really want to go back to the Taylor place just now, but I didn't want Jase to think I was chicken, so I waved at Mr. Pearcy and he motioned me to his side of the street. The grinning skull flashed into my mind for an instant. I might tell Jase about it later, but right now didn't seem the time. Besides, it was just Mr. Pearcy. That other thing was that it wasn't real. It was just my imagination.

"It was a good TV dinner," he said without preamble. "You need a job, girl?"

I didn't know what to say. Adults were not usually so direct. "I——yeah. Maybe."

He laughed. "I could use someone to straighten up the place." He leaned toward me and whispered, "And I need someone to show me some things in the kitchen."

"Sure," I replied. "I'll have to ask my Gramps though."

He nodded and headed back to his porch. "Only be a couple times a week. Won't interfere with your schoolin' or nothing like that." He took his chair and sat facing the street. "I'll pay ya."

"Okay, I'll check with Gramps." A little worm of excitement curled in my belly. I *did* like to have my own money. "I'll come by tomorrow and tell you."

With another little wave of his hand, he stood up to go inside.

I glanced back as the screen door was closing, and for just a moment I could swear...no, it was just the light. He wasn't bald. His hair was gray, but his head was *not* smooth and bone white with just a few grotty wisps of hair clinging to it.

Jase and Lady were waiting for me across the street. "You got a job?" he asked.

I pushed the strange image away and grinned. "Maybe."

"Well," he said. "I'm impressed. That's what I need. I mow grass in the summer, but an after school job could be cool. Wonder if the old man needs me for anything?"

"I'll ask him," I said. "No harm in asking, is there?"

We pedaled on toward the Taylor place. No one other than Mr. Pearcy lived very close to the old house. It had a long, wide, yard and the fence was black wrought iron with those spiky points on the top of each post. The house itself crouched toward the rear of the deep lot.

I stopped my bike. "Do you really wanna go in?"

In answer, he leaned over, opened the screechy gate, and walked his bike right through before he halted. "It doesn't seem as much fun as it used to. You know, my buddy, Billy Bob, he always wants to come here. Then he gets on the front porch and has an asthma attack or something. I don't know anyone who's been upstairs, do you?"

"No. Karla and I couldn't even get up the nerve to go up to the door." I glanced up at the roofline just in time to catch a glimpse of the curtain fluttering at the second story window as if there was a breeze inside the room. Maybe there was a hole in the attic or something.

"You did go in, though," Jase said. "All by yourself." I fancied I heard a note of respect in his voice.

"I really miss Karla," I replied. Then I turned my bike toward home. I didn't want to go into that dusty old place again. I wanted Karla back so she could do it with me, or even with Jase and me.

He didn't argue. But when he was almost out of the gate, it suddenly flew out of his grasp and slammed his ankle between the sharp bottom-edge and the solid metal post.

"Ow!" His voice cracked like glass.

I dropped my bike and ran to help.

Lady was already there, nosing at his hand, the one covering

the wound. "Oh, man!" He gritted his teeth against the pain.
"That iron gate is heavy." He limped his bike over to the same
bench we'd sat on last time and pulled up his jeans to examine
the ankle. Blood was welling up into the gash. As I watched, it
spilled over, soaking into the cuff of his sock.

I leaned down. "That looks deep."

He glanced around for something to put on it, but there was
nothing. He pulled his sock up to cover it, then slapped at something on the back of his neck. Without knowing why, I glanced
up at the second-floor window. It was in shadow now, but I
couldn't see anything moving. I felt something though, and just
like Jase, I slapped the back of my neck because the skin there
was suddenly crawly with something. I hoped it was just sweat,
but when I pulled my hand away it was covered with tiny flies.

"Yuck!" I shook the insects off and looked at Jase. His neck
was crawling with them, too. He began to swat at himself and I
saw that the flies were swarming around the bloody cut on
his leg.

"C'mon," I yelled. "I've got band-aids at my house." I climbed
back on my bike and took off. We outran the flies easily. When I
looked over my shoulder, I could see them still swarming, just
outside the old garage at the side of the house.

Gramps was home when we got there. "What happened?" he
asked as I held the door open for Jase who was limping
noticeably.

"Piece of metal," I said. I don't know why I didn't tell the
whole truth. Yes, I do. He wouldn't want me even going inside
the fence of the old Taylor place. I could imagine exactly what
he'd say. "Got no business in there. 'S private property—ain't
ours." But I didn't lie, not exactly. And if he came right out and
asked me, I'd tell him the truth. I was pretty sure of it.

Gramps leaned over just like I had, and Jase pulled up his

jeans leg and peeled down his bloody sock. "Had your tetanus shot?" Gramps asked.

"Yes, sir." Jase gritted his teeth again as Gramps pulled some cotton sock fibers out of the gash. "We all got 'em after Rodney Jones, you know, last year."

"'S right," Gramps said. "Terrible, terrible thing, lockjaw." He went ahead and pulled the sock right off Jase's foot. I could tell Jase was embarrassed so I left the room.

"I'm running water in the tub," I said. "I'll get the peroxide, too."

Gramps grunted his agreement then I heard him say, "Don't think it needs stitches, but we'll know for sure when we get it cleaned up." Then he came in with Jase hopping on his good foot. I think he was trying to keep from getting blood on the linoleum.

He stuck his other foot under the faucet in the tub and washed it with soap and warm water. After it was clean it didn't look so bad. Jase did all the important stuff himself—poured it full of peroxide and then slapped a big band-aid on it after it dried. While he did that, I brought Lady inside. She was staring in through the storm door as if we were torturing her master.

"That looks like a good dog." Gramps held out his hand just like I'd done earlier, and Lady gave him a lick of approval, too. "Maybe we *do* need a dog."

I'd been after him to let me have a dog forever. He always said he didn't have time to train one. He'd had an old dog named Black Bart when he was a kid. Gran said he never got over the horrific way Bart died, crushed to death under Great-Grampa's tractor. I don't think Gramps ever forgave his dad for that, even though it was an accident. Gran said that was the reason he never wanted another dog.

Once he was cleaned up and the gash was covered, Jase was

ready to go home. I told Gramps I'd better ride along, too, and he let me, grudgingly.

I think Gramps was more worried about Lady having to run along behind us the whole way, but Jase put his mind at ease when he explained that sometimes Lady took shortcuts through fields and places we couldn't go on our bikes.

"Sometimes she beats me home," he said seriously.

Gramps was all right with that, and made me promise to be home before supper. Then we all sat down to a lunch of bologna and tomato sandwiches, another of Gramps's conditions for letting me go. I was surprised when Jase stood up and started cleaning off the table when we were finished. Lady didn't beg or anything. Gramps gave her the heel of the bologna when he thought we weren't looking.

He walked out on the front porch as we were climbing onto our bikes, hooking his thumbs into his front pockets and looking at the horizon thoughtfully. "Ya know, that old Taylor place is sort of like a magnet. Don't let it draw you in." He looked right at us. "Rennie Taylor died there. She fell down the stairs and broke her neck, so they say."

Shivers ran up my back and I thought I saw Jase shake himself a bit. "When was that?" I asked.

Gramps looked at me, hard. I didn't think he was going to answer. Finally, he said, "Long time ago, Sprout. Long time ago." Then he turned on his heel and disappeared into the cool recesses of the house.

4

The ride to Jase's house wasn't nearly as long as I thought it would be. We started playing a whistling game. He would whistle a song and I would have to guess the name of it. If I guessed correctly, then I got to whistle one. But if I got it wrong, he got to go again. He stumped me on *Wooly Bully*, but I stumped him on *Tequila*. I felt a little guilty doing that one. I kept giggling and messing it up. It was one of Gramps's favorite sing-a-long songs.

In no time at all, we were riding up his long curving drive. The big gate was already open. Jase said they never closed it unless they were going to be away overnight or something.

I was a little bit leery when I realized no one was home. I trusted Jase, but still, he was a boy and I'd never had a boy for a real *friend* before. Several had chased me at recess over the years, and Cody Stevens sent Darla over to my desk one day to ask me if I liked him, but I thought it was a joke so I just said not really. In truth, I had the biggest crush on him. Who didn't? He was the class star, the athlete, and the one who was always the captain at whatever game we were playing in our PE class. But he wasn't overly bright. He was in the red robin reading group and that was the lowest. Still, I didn't hold that against him. I knew very few kids who liked to read as much as I did.

But really, if he'd been very bright he wouldn't have sent snooty old Darla over to my desk. She didn't like me and I didn't care one whit about her either. So I just said *not really* because I thought she would say something ugly like, "Oh, you do like him? Well, too bad 'cause he wanted me to tell you woof-woof," or something like that. After all, she's the one who complimented me on having such long eyelashes one day and then when I said thank you, she said, "I figured they were false. No one has real eyelashes like that." And then she'd flounced back to her seat and left me sitting there confused, not sure if I'd been complimented or burned.

Later, I thought up all kinds of good comebacks: "False eyelashes? You mean like the falsies you wear in your bra?" or "My eyelashes? Sure, they're real. Aren't yours? Wait, I'm sorry. Where *are* yours?" But I could never speak up when I needed to. It always took me half the next day to come up with anything remotely clever or hurtful. Gramps says it's because I'm just basically a nice person. Nice and boring. And *suspicious*.

Because of my suspicious nature, I made Cody mad or hurt his feelings or something, because he never spoke to me again. Ever. Except on Valentine's Day when he stuffed a card in my box that said, "You broke my heart, Valentine!" And it showed a big red heart with a band-aid on it sort of like the one on Jase's ankle. Cody didn't sign the card, though. If I hadn't been looking, I never would have known it had come from him. Later that year, he gave Darla his ID bracelet and she let him kiss her under the bleachers after school.

Jase held the door open for me and sure enough, there was Lady, stretched out on the kitchen floor. "How'd she get in?" I asked. He'd already told me his folks were in Lubbock for the day at some kind of church meeting about ending the war.

He motioned toward the screen door leading out of the kitchen. The bottom of the door had a slight, paw-sized gap. "She's opened it so many times it sort of got sprung. Now, even if it's latched, she can still get it open far enough to squeeze inside." He shrugged and motioned me to follow him.

In the living room his folks had a record player in one of those big coffin-sized cabinets. The front was a TV screen with a silver twist knob, and then you opened the lid and it was a whole stereo complete with a radio and record player.

"Wow." I was impressed. "That's pretty fancy," I said.

Jase couldn't hide his grin. He pulled up the center of the turntable so that a 45 would play, then he put my record on and set the needle into the first groove.

The beginning of *Crimson and Clover* floated into the room. I was just about to comment on how wonderful it sounded when *Wham!* The record flew off the turntable and smacked me right square in the forehead.

The music blared out of the speaker at top volume *even without the record*, but it didn't sound like Tommy James anymore. It sounded like something dark and loud and huge.

"Jase!" I screamed. I tried to run, hit the wall, and slid down it to the floor. Stunned, I lay crumpled near the baseboard, afraid to move, afraid not to.

He dashed across the room and pulled me up to a sitting position.

"What happened?" I shouted. The music was *still* blaring. Lady was standing in the doorway between the living room and kitchen. All at once, she stuck her snout into the air and howled like a coyote. It was a long mournful note and it ended with a series of short little yips that would have been comical if I hadn't seen the strange look in her eyes. She looked as if the howl was directed at something—or someone—near the ceiling. Her eyes were locked on a spot almost directly above me in the corner of the living room.

Dragging me with him, Jase hurried to the stereo and picked up the record arm, thus removing the scratching needle from the bare turntable. For a moment, the music continued playing, and then it quit. And somehow the silence, filled only by the yipping howl, was even worse.

I covered my ears with both hands and shut my eyes. Jase tapped me on the shoulder. "I'm sorry," he said.

At least I think that's what he said. I uncovered my ears cautiously.

"Are you all right?"

I nodded. Tomorrow my neck would be so stiff I could barely turn my head, but right then, I didn't feel anything except a little ding in the middle of my forehead where the edge of the 45 had hit me. I must have been rubbing it unconsciously. Jase pushed my bangs up and examined it.

"It's really red," he said. "But at least it's not bleeding."

I wondered if he was thinking the same thing I was: *Now we're both marked.*

Then the music started up again with a violent beat. Jase looked at the record in his hand, then he looked at me and we both took off running toward the back door. We didn't stop until we were far enough away from the house that we couldn't hear the music anymore.

At last, I stopped and bent over at the waist, trying to catch my breath from being smacked with a record and then doing the fifty-yard dash to get away from music that *would not stop playing.* Jase halted a little further along and then he bent over, too. When we looked back, Lady was standing in the yard between the house and us. She looked odd standing there like a statue. I don't know why I thought she would just naturally follow us, but at least she wasn't howling anymore.

"I don't think I can go back in there," I said, holding one hand to the stitch in my side as my breathing grew easier.

"Me either...but I gotta live there." Jase's voice was shrill, and the way he waved his hands around when he said it struck me as funny and I began to laugh. After a moment, he joined in and we both stood there laughing and gasping for breath until we finally had to sit down right there in the field and wait for the moment to pass.

At last, he stood up. "I'm going back in."

I stood up, too, and dusted off the seat of my jeans. He gave my braid a tug and we grinned at each other gamely.

That's when it began to rain, right out of the clear blue sky. The rain was not water, but tiny balls of gray jelly. They stuck to our clothes, tangled in our hair, and sizzled when they touched our skin, but they didn't burn. At least I didn't think they had, until I looked at Jase and he looked at me and our mouths fell open at the same time. Both our faces were dotted with little round marks the exact size and color of pencil erasers.

Lady had high-tailed it for the barn as soon as the drops started to fall. She knew this wasn't your typical cats-and-dogs type rain.

"What is it?" I shouted as we dashed toward the barn.

Jase just shook his head and motioned for me to hurry. All around us the prairie grass was bending under the weight of the globs of jelly. The ground was beginning to smoke. I guessed they were burning somehow, just like the marks on our faces, but how? There was no heat, no sensation of fire.

"Maybe it's some sort of chemical reaction," Jase said as we washed ourselves with rags dipped in the horse trough under the barn's overhang.

That made sense to me, at least as much sense as anything else. "Where do you think it came from?"

"There's a chemical plant down by Ozona. Maybe it's

from there."

I bathed my face and neck over and over. For a moment I worried about horse germs, saliva or something, but then I thought *who cares* and just closed my eyes. The liquid was so cool sliding down my skin. When I opened my eyes, Jase was staring at me. "What?" I asked. "Is it worse? Are the spots getting worse?" I let the rag fall to my side, my other hand creeping across my cheeks in search of clues.

"No," he said. "It isn't that." His face reddened which made the spots stand out even more.

"Then what is it?" Alarm crept into my voice. Could this day get any stranger? What was on me now? I began to rub at my face. It was as if I could actually feel something there, something alive.

"No, no, no." Jase grabbed my hands. "Stop! You're hurting yourself."

I felt tears spring up in my eyes. I hated when that happened. What was wrong with me today? Maybe it was just all the weird tension caused by the fear. "What is it?" My voice trembled. Jase still had hold of my hands.

"Nothing," he released my wrists. "You just, you're so—"

Behind us, Lady sneezed violently. Apparently she'd dashed into the loose hay to hide.

Now it was my turn to blush. I wanted to turn away, but I couldn't. "I'm all spotted," I whispered. "Like you."

Jase leaned in and gently bonked foreheads with me, carefully avoiding the place where the record had hit me, and then he gave my braid another little tug and strode away.

"There ya go, Spot," he chuckled. He took off toward the field. The gooey rain had stopped as suddenly as it began.

I didn't know what to say. But for a moment, I felt very different. Strange. I'd forgotten everything that happened.

He stopped in the middle of the smoking field and said,

"This is where it crashed. Right here." I could see it then, the deep wound the plane had gouged into the soft flesh of the earth, the telling-scar where the grass was dead or missing altogether.

Jase and I stood side-by-side looking at the aftermath. "Do you think *he's* making this stuff happen?" I asked.

He shook his head. "Nothing like this happened before. He would just come and stare at me in my room, or in my window." He shuddered visibly and the wind kicked up a notch. I saw Lady peek out from under the pile of straw in the wide-open barn.

"So it's me, huh? He doesn't like me or something."

His next words were whisked away from his lips. I didn't hear what he said. I cupped my hand around my ear. "What?"

He leaned in close. "I said, you better get home. It looks like a *real* storm is coming!" Far out in the field stood Jase's horse, Buddy.

"He won't come near the crash site," he said.

Sure enough, in moments I saw the pretty palomino galloping toward the barn along the fence line and as far away from us as possible. I wondered if he'd been hit with the jelly blobs. But I didn't have time to mention it to Jase.

The sky was blackening, the clouds scudding across the afternoon as though they were late for an appointment some-where else. "I guess you're right. I'd better go." Jase nodded and motioned toward the side of the house. Apparently, he didn't want to chance going back through the living room.

I was sitting safely on my bike, the weather had calmed down, and Lady had crept out of hiding. "Want me to go in and find your 45?" he asked.

I shook my head vehemently. "I don't care if I ever see that record again." My fingers strayed to the tender spot on my fore-head. "Come home with me," I blurted.

Jase cocked his head the way I'd seen Lady do when she was trying to understand something. "I'll be okay," he said. "My folks should be on their way home, and besides, like I said, Mr. Gilpin never acted like this before."

"Gilpin? Who's that?"

"That's the pilot's name, Roger Gilpin. Didn't I tell you?" He flipped his hair back, a gesture I'd come to recognize as pure nervousness.

"How'd you find that out?" *And what else have you not told me?*

He glanced at the hanging clouds, his hand straying down to Lady's smooth head as if for reassurance. "My dad was so freaked out after he got home that night that he went to the Sheriff's Office and demanded to see the report."

"That makes sense. They weren't here when it happened so I'm sure they were upset."

A dark look clouded his face, as if a corner of the stormy sky had fallen on him. "Yeah, they're always somewhere else lately."

I kicked my bike pedal aimlessly, trying to imagine what my Gramps would say, or do, if I told him I thought some guy was haunting my room. No way of knowing, I guess. But I thought he'd at least try to find out what was happening. Funny, you just never know what someone is carrying around when you only sit by him or her in school or pass them occasionally in the hall. I'd always thought Jase was so cool and laid back. It turned out he was just like the rest of us—full of doubt and fear.

"So," he hesitated. "You got any ideas about any of this stuff?"

I couldn't believe he still thought I might know what to do. "No, but I do think we need some help. We don't even know for sure what we're dealing with."

"You mean adult help?"

"I guess."

"But I already tried my folks, remember."

"Yeah, but I was thinking more like a preacher or a priest."

His face lit up. "Yeah! See I knew you'd think of something. Surely someone like that will know what to do." But then his face clouded over again. "I can't ask our preacher, though. He'd tell my folks and then I'd get in trouble for involving someone else in our family problem. You know, since Dad already told me to quit being such a sissy."

I felt myself nodding the whole time, but I wasn't listening very carefully. "Well, I don't go to church at all so no help there, but aren't there priests who are supposed to help with this sort of thing? I mean holy water and stuff like that?"

"Yeah! Billy Bob once said his grandma kept a whole bottle of the stuff on her bedroom dresser. We'll get him to bring us some. Then what do we do with it?"

I laughed. He'd been so animated for a moment there. "Let me research it some more. I think you just sort of sprinkle it around and it makes the spirit leave or something."

Jase patted me on the shoulder like he'd been patting Lady on the head. "Good! Good!" I thought he was going to give me a treat there for a minute, maybe a milk bone or two. "That will probably work," he continued. "I'm going to go in and give Bill a call. You want to wait and see what he says?" We both glanced up at the glowering sky.

"Guess not. I'd better ride."

"Hold on." He ran back and grabbed his bike. "I'm going to ride with you at least part of the way." Lady perked up and away we went.

I was glad he was going with me. The storm clouds had quit blowing around, and that seemed even more ominous. Now it felt like they were directly overhead. If they started spitting those jelly balls again, I didn't know what we'd do. *Gotta get to the public library as soon as possible.* "Hey!"

Jase looked at me across the short gap between our bikes.

"Feel like a trip to the library?" I could see him debating in his head. "Maybe we could find out more about holy water and ghosts."

He nodded. "I wanna call Billy Bob, too, though. The sooner we get holy water, the better I'll feel."

That made sense. I kept forgetting that he had to sleep in that crazy house. "Yeah. You go and do that and I will stop by the library and see what I can dig up."

He rode with me all the way to the library. Lady, too. "I'm just going to go by Bill's house," he said as we parted. "He only lives a few blocks from here."

"Okay," I said. "Will you call me or something when you find out about the holy water?"

"Sure."

"My number's 3454." We only had to dial a 2 and then our four-digit number. It was a small town so everyone had the same prefix.

He smiled. "That's easy to remember."

I nodded. "Jase?"

"Yeah?"

"I'm sorry we didn't get to listen to your album." I looked up at the brick and glass-block front of the small library. It was my absolute second favorite place in the world. My first place being my own front yard.

Jase threw his head back and laughed. "I wonder where it is?" He looked at me seriously. "I'm sort of afraid to even play it now. It might take my head clean off!"

"I don't think it was mad at you—whatever *it* is."

He sat rocking his bike back and forth, thinking.

A woman with two little kids walked up the sidewalk toward us. "Don't wanna!" the little boy was saying. He kept trying to pull away from his mother. But the little girl was skipping ahead, probably headed to her favorite place just like me.

"Why would Mr. Gilpin's ghost," he glanced at me when he

said the g-word, "that is what we're both thinking right?"

I nodded.

"Why would he be mad at you for trying to help me?"

A light bulb clicked on in my brain. "Because I'm trying to help you get rid of him!" I pulled my own braid, brown and thick with melting gray jelly, around to the front and chewed on the end of it as I continued to put the clues together. "He's here for some reason, and he wants you to help him. That's why he keeps hanging around you."

Jase was looking at me in awe. "See! I knew you could help me figure this stuff out." His face was almost beaming. "So, what do you think he wants me to help him do?"

I sort of shrugged. One of the cops my Gramps worked with was driving by. He raised his hand and I raised mine back. They all watched after me. I guess Gramps told them to. He worried about me, a lot. When it was clear again, I said, "Didn't you say that Lady escorted the pilot, Mr. Gilpin, off into the field that first night?"

"Yeah. Well, I wrote that in my story."

I parked my bike in the rack near the front door. "Then maybe he's looking for something in that field. Maybe we need to go back and look some more. That jelly-rain sort of scared us off, didn't it?"

Jase still sat on his bike. "Yeah, something scared us out of the house, then scared us out of the field." He looked at me with admiration. "Something sure is trying to scare you away. None of that happened before you got there."

I grimaced. "Yeah, I think we established that already." I didn't know whether to feel hurt or flattered. "But I know one good thing."

He raised his eyebrows questioningly.

I was looking at my reflection in the glass front of the library. "At least we're not spotted anymore!"

5

That night the phone rang and it was for me. I never got calls now, since Karla moved. I just didn't connect with anyone any more and didn't want to, I guess. But this time it was Jase.

Gramps held the receiver out, and I took the whole phone and pulled it into the utility closet in the hallway and shut the door. Gramps walked away with no questions asked. At least I think he did, it sounded like he did.

"So, did you talk to Billy Bob?" I didn't believe in small talk.

Jase chuckled. He was speaking in a low voice just like me. "Yep. He's all for it."

"Can we get some holy water?" I got a sudden vision of Gramps standing outside my door, listening, so I held my breath and yanked it open, but no one was there. I wasn't good at this sneaky stuff. Didn't even like it.

"Yeah, pretty sure we can. What'd you find out at the library?"

I took a deep breath. "Well, I looked at a lot of books on ghosts and spirits and stuff and it's kind of like we thought. Sometimes if a person dies suddenly, or tragically, his or her spirit might not be able to cross over to the other side. They just sort of get stuck hanging around."

"Well..." Jase was silent for a moment. "First of all, why do they get stuck? Second, how do we get rid of them or help them cross or whatever, and third...can they hurt us?"

I laughed and touched the sore spot on my forehead. "First, I don't know. Second, holy water *and* figuring out what is keeping them here, and third, the knot on my forehead says yes, they can hurt us."

Jase was so silent I thought he'd hung up on me.

"You still there?" My heart was loud in the enclosed space of the utility closet surrounded by the broom, mop, and ironing board.

"I'm here," he said. "I—uh. I didn't mean for you to get hurt."

I laughed again. "It's okay. It's almost gone anyway. Besides, except for the weirdness, you know flying records and jellyfish-poop from above, I had a pretty good time today."

"Me, too." His rejoinder was immediate so I was fairly sure he was telling the truth and not just trying to make me feel better. "But still, I think tomorrow it'll be just me and Billy Bob. We'll go get some of his Grandma's holy water and then go to my house and see what happens."

I couldn't believe he was saying that. It was like I was being excluded from the boys-only club or something. I tried not to let my hurt feelings show up in my voice though. "Oh. Okay, I understand."

"I'll call you after, you know, whatever happens. Okay?"

"Sure." I couldn't help it. My feelings *were* hurt. "I gotta go. Gotta wash dishes." I hung up the phone before the catch in my throat swallowed my voice. I didn't even get a chance to tell him what I'd found out about flies, how they are somehow attracted to evil spirits. And how ghosts won't usually try to hurt you, but shadow men and evil spirits will.

I'd thought Jase might be my first real friend since Karla. I missed her so much. We did the dumbest things together, like spreading an old blanket in the middle of the yard after dark so we could try to count the stars. One of us would always get mixed up and get the giggles. Then we'd have to start all over. It wasn't a big deal, but it was fun. We'd lie there and talk about boys and movie stars like Leonard Whiting from *Romeo and Juliet*, or TV stars like Bobby Sherman. We thought they were both *so* cute. Of course, we each had our favorite Monkee and Beatle, too. Hers were Davy and Paul, mine were Davy and George. We extolled all their many virtues several times over. Sometimes we'd get brave and tell each other spooky stories, and dare each other to go in the old Taylor place.

Now she was off in California, a million miles away, and I was stuck here in Crossroads all alone except for two boys and a ghost, none of who seemed to want me around.

I ran a hot bath, blubbering the whole time I was soaking, and then I felt better. I vowed to write Karla a long letter before bedtime, and let her in on all the stuff going on with the Taylor place and Mr. Gilpin. I was pretty sure she'd think I was just making it all up.

Would I tell her about how the boys suddenly decided I was no longer welcome or helpful? Probably. Then on Monday, maybe I'd start looking for a new friend at school. Maybe Shelby Rose. She was nice. Or Laura Gonzales. She was quiet like me. There had to be somebody to hang around with besides *boys*.

SUNDAY DRAGGED. Gramps didn't have to work so we made breakfast together. Pancakes, bacon, and lots of butter and syrup, milk for me, and coffee for Gramps. While we ate, I told him about the job offer from Mr. Pearcy.

"You want to try it?" he asked. "It's a big responsibility,

agreeing to be somewhere at the same time on the same day each week. People get dependent on you."

"Yeah? I hadn't thought of it like that." I played with my braid. I'd washed my hair twice to get all the gray goo out of it last night. I tried to decide if he wanted me to take the job, or if he thought I couldn't handle it.

"Big responsibility," he repeated. "Sure you're ready for that?"

I thought about coming home to the empty house after school like I'd been doing lately. Gramps got home as soon as he could, I knew that, but it still got lonely sometimes. "Yeah, I think I'd like to talk to him about it. Maybe it'll be okay. He seemed awfully lost at the grocery store."

Gramps placed his hands on either side of his plate. He pushed the plate back and forth with his two thumbs. "Don't know what I would've done without you after Gran got sick." He picked up the plate and put it in the sink. "I guess I can share you a bit." He ruffled my bangs and stepped out the backdoor into the Sunday morning sunshine.

I followed him onto the porch. He sat in his rocker and I sat in the porch swing.

"What'cha thinking about?"

He was just about to put a pinch of snuff in his lip, but he hesitated. "You really want to know?"

"Yes," I replied. I don't know what I was hoping he would say. Something to make me feel better about all the odd stuff that had happened, maybe. Or something to make me feel better about boys if nothing else.

I kicked my feet under the swing, pushed too hard, and made it bounce on its chains. Gramps hated when I did that. I put my feet down carefully.

He just sat there a moment. Then he stuck the snuff in his mouth and sat some more. "Your grandma was the love of my life," he said. "I miss her terribly. I used to think she was still around." He stopped talking for a while, his thoughts obviously deep in the past. "I'd think I heard her voice or I'd walk into the bedroom and her favorite book would be open on the nightstand."

I waited patiently. I remembered some of this. He'd even asked me about the book a time or two. But he'd never said why he had wanted to know. He just asked if I had put it there.

He sat back in the old rocker. "I don't feel her anymore."

I started to protest, to say I was sure she was still around. Then I thought about how I didn't feel her or Mom anymore. "You think she's gone on now?"

Gramps nodded. He seemed relieved that I'd accepted his answer so readily. "I think she's resting now," he said. "She doesn't have to stick around and look after us." He smiled. "I think she stayed around long enough to make sure I was taking care of you properly."

I laughed out loud. That did sound like my Gran, always worrying about others. "So what would make a person stick around, you know, after they passed away?" I tucked the end of my braid into the corner of my mouth and waited to see if he understood the question.

"Like a ghost, you mean?" He didn't look at me.

"Yeah, or an evil spirit or something." I'd read about shadow men, but just thinking about them made me cringe. I didn't want to talk about them out loud. Not with Gramps. Maybe I could have with Jase. If he hadn't deserted me.

Gramps's eyes were mild blue. He looked at the street just beyond our porch, but I knew he was seeing a different place as he spoke. "I don't believe I've ever encountered an evil *spirit*," he said. "But I've certainly encountered lots of evil people in my line of work, when I was a regular officer."

He'd told me that before, how he thought some people must

have evil natures or something, in order to account for the things they did.

He shrugged. "So, in my opinion, if some people are good and some are evil, and if the good people can stick around to make sure their business is finished, like Gran did, then I suppose I would also have to believe that evil people can stick around, too."

"Until their business is finished," I murmured.

We were both quiet again. It was the first time we'd ever talked about death or what we thought happened afterward. "So, you think Mama and Gran are resting now?"

He rocked back and forth a few times before he answered. "They were both wonderful people. I know they are," he said confidently. "They deserve to rest."

I got up and moved to Gramps's lap the way I hadn't done in quite a while. "I miss them, too."

He hugged me so tight I swear I felt a rib crack. "We've got each other," he said. "We've always got each other."

Of course, I hugged him right back.

"You having some kind of nightmares or something, Sprout?"

I nodded. "Yeah, something like that." Then I took a chance. "You know any tricks to get rid of ghostly nightmares?"

He leaned over and spit a brown stream of snuff juice into the blue and purple four o'clocks. Gran would've scolded him harshly for that if she'd been here. "Best cure for anything scary is to never let on that you're afraid. Fake it if you have to. That's where most courage begins anyhow."

I was surprised. It wasn't what I'd expected him to say. Then I wanted to ask him if he'd ever had to fake being brave, but I was pretty sure I knew the answer. At Mama's funeral, and then at Gran's, he had stood stoically holding my hand, eyes shimmering with unshed tears. But he'd never fallen apart, not where I could see at least. If that wasn't courage, it would do for now.

I stood up and leapt off the porch. I'd heard enough. "I'm going over to Mr. Pearcy's house and see if he needs anything."

Gramps leaned over and spit another stream of snuff into the flowers. I thought I heard him chuckling a bit when I retrieved my bike from the garage.

I rode the three blocks to Mr. Pearcy's house, all the while thinking how nice it would be to have a dog like Lady loping along beside me, keeping me company.

Mr. Pearcy wasn't home. Probably still at church. I walked around the house to see if there was anything outside that needed to be done. Jase had asked me to see if Mr. Pearcy needed a boy to help him in the yard or anything, but now I wasn't sure if I wanted to ask for Jase anymore. He didn't want my help after he got Billy Bob. Why should I help him get a job?

Just then, Mr. Pearcy drove up in his big white Oldsmobile. I raised my hand in greeting, and he nodded curtly.

"Hello," I said as soon as he stepped out of the car. "I'm here to see if you need me to start working today."

He stared at me so long and so hard that I became aware of a mockingbird singing in the fruitless mulberry tree above my head. I shuffled my feet in the grass and wondered what I'd done, or said, that was wrong. "If it's a bad time—"

"C'mon in the house," he replied at last. "No working on Sunday, but we can talk about it over a glass of iced tea, I guess. Although it's the instant kind. Don't know how to make brewed. Never comes out the same as when Mary made it." He said all that as we were walking up the porch. He held open the front door and I stepped inside. The house was rather dark and a bit dusty. Not too bad, but it did need some attention.

"I'd be glad to brew up some fresh tea if you'd like. I can show you how to do it too." I still felt funny telling a grown up I knew how to do something better than he did, but that's what he said he needed.

"Kitchen's this way." He pointed ahead, straight through the living room.

I took the initiative and plowed on ahead. "I hope you have some tea bags and sugar," I offered. "And a small saucepan or tea kettle."

He stepped to the cupboard and pulled out a small pan and set it on the stove. Then he opened the pantry door, took tea bags from a clear glass container, and then pointed to the sugar in the matched set of canisters on the long counter. The set contained four canisters, each one painted with a beautiful picture of a different flower. The sugar was in the pink tulip container. He also placed a fat glass pitcher on the counter.

"Just fill the pan half full of water." I did this while speaking. "Put two tea bags into it like this, with the strings hanging over so you can pull them out when it's done, then put the pan on the burner and turn it to high heat. When it begins to boil, turn off the heat and let the tea sit there and steep for a few minutes while you fill the tea pitcher almost full of water, and about a half cup of sugar. The longer you let the tea sit and steep with the tea bags still in the water, the stronger it will taste." I took the pan off the burner and lifted out the tea bags by their strings. Then I poured the tea into the pitcher and stirred until all the sugar was dissolved. "'Course, you don't have to make it that sweet. I'm just doing it the way we drink it at home."

Mr. Pearcy had watched the whole thing without saying a word. He took two glasses from the cupboard and filled them with ice from the metal trays in the freezer. I poured the amber colored liquid into the glasses. I was getting nervous. The skull thing was in the back of my mind, but I knew that was ridiculous. It was just Mr. Pearcy, that's all. "Do you have lemons or limes?"

He shook his head and downed half his glass of tea in one long drink. "Ahhh," he breathed. "Perfect."

"I'm glad you don't think it's too sweet. My Gramps likes his tea like syrup." I took a long drink. It was good. I felt proud. And there was nothing to be nervous about, nothing at all.

"You're hired," Mr. Pearcy said. Then he drained his glass and held it out to me for a refill.

I grinned at him, refilled his glass, and placed the pitcher in the refrigerator. Then I turned to the sink and rinsed the pan and the wooden spoon and placed them in the dish drainer. He was keeping the kitchen pretty neat. I figured after I showed him how to fix a few simple meals, he probably wouldn't even need me anymore.

"Let's go in here and talk wages," he said.

We sat at the dining room table and he pushed a tablet of paper toward me. "I want you to help me figure out what I can cook and what I need to buy."

I sat looking at the paper and tapping the pencil against my chin. We discussed his likes and dislikes and I wound up making a short list of bacon, eggs, pancake mix, sandwich makings, and pork chops. I added potatoes, a few canned vegetables, and a few TV dinners. I figured he could learn a few breakfast things easy enough, plus one dinner item, the pork chops, and he would just have to eat sandwiches in between my visits. Three days a week, after school, he said. Plus Saturday if I wanted.

He said the only thing he really needed help with besides cooking was washing clothes. "How do you sort them?" he asked. "I know Mary didn't just throw everything in the machine all at once."

I didn't laugh. My Gran had been teaching me housekeeping rules ever since I was old enough to stand on a stool and help her. She also taught me how to cook. It was as if she knew that one day I would be taking care of myself *and* others. Sometimes

I think she knew she wasn't going to be around that much longer. I turned my head to the side and pretended to cough so that Mr. Pearcy wouldn't know that just thinking about my Gran sometimes made me cry. I was the same way about my mama until Gran passed away. Then I guess one grief replaced the other. I wondered if he did the same thing when he thought about his Mary.

"Well," I began. "The main thing is just to keep your dark clothes away from your light ones. Always wash the towels and sheets in hot water and—"

He pushed the tablet at me. "Write it, please." His eyes were full of water. "I'll never remember." He wiped a broad thumb under each eye. "And would you write down the settings for me, too? What goes in cold, what goes in hot, or warm?"

"Sure." I made a simple list then I thought of something. "If I'm coming three times a week to cook, why don't I just do the laundry then?"

Pulling a handkerchief from his pocket, he wiped his eyes and took a deep breath. "You can help, but I need to learn these things for myself."

I nodded. "Of course and, Mr. Pearcy?"

He looked at me solemnly.

"You can call me if you need to, anytime." I wrote my phone number at the bottom of the laundry instructions. Then I almost laughed. I'd given out my phone number more the last two days than I had in the last two years.

I must have been smiling because he said, "Your Grampa's okay with this arrangement?"

"Yes. He said he could share me. I sort of help him do all this stuff at home, too. You know, since my Gran passed on and everything."

His hanky came out again. "I am sorry, girl," he said. "I

mean, Stevie. I just can't seem to get used to the idea that my Mary isn't coming back."

I wanted to go over and give him a hug like I did my own Gramps, but I'd just barely got used to the idea of telling him how to do things. I didn't think I was allowed to hug him, even if I had known him all my life. "It's okay," I said. "I still miss my Gran all the time. And my mom, too."

"You've had your share of heartache, haven't you?" His voice was a little shaky, but I thought it was getting stronger.

"I've still got my Gramps," I said. I never wanted people to feel sorry for me. The kids at school tried that, after my mom was killed in that car wreck. They hemmed me up in the corner the day after I came back to school. They wanted me to tell them what it was like to bury your mom. Then they wanted to pat me and watch me cry, but I didn't let them. I poked Johnny Stillwell in the stomach when he wouldn't get out of the way and let me out of that corner. No one messed with me after that, except Karla. But she didn't question me. She just walked along beside me at lunchtime and then after awhile she took my hand and pulled me to the bleachers where we sat and talked for the rest of the period.

"So," I stood up. "Would you like for me to help you cook something right now?"

He went back to the kitchen and rooted around in the pantry, then the freezer. "I've got another one of those TV dinners for tonight," he called. "The ladies at church fed me lunch."

I stood in the door watching him inventory his kitchen.

"I'll go tomorrow and get the groceries you recommended." He pointed to the first list I'd made.

"Okay, then I'll be over after school and we'll do some cooking."

"Wait."

I was about to go out the door, but I turned back when he called. Beside the front door, there was a small table with several framed photographs on it. One of the pictures was obviously Mr. and Mrs. Pearcy, though they were quite a bit younger. And the other photo was of a nice looking couple with two smiling children.

He must have noticed me looking at the pictures. "My son and his family," he explained proudly. "They live over in Lubbock. They're coming to visit next weekend. And then I'm going to go and visit them next time. Maybe see my grandson play football. He's just about your age you know."

"That's great. I'll bet you'll have a really nice visit. I know I'd miss my Gramps if I couldn't see him all the time."

"Well, I called you back because we didn't discuss your wages." His face was merry. I could tell he was going to tease me in some way. So I decided to get him first.

"I only charge ten dollars an hour," I said seriously. Then I burst out laughing. His face had gone from merry to shocked in the blink of an eye. "I'm teasing, Mr. Pearcy! I've never even had a job before."

Relief flooded his features and he shook his finger at me mock-sternly. "I'm going to have to keep my eye on you!"

I could tell he didn't mind a little teasing. It's how my Gramps and I were with each other.

"How about fifty cents an hour?"

Now I was the one grinning. I hoped he wasn't teasing me because if I made fifty cents an hour, that would mean I might earn a whole dollar every time I came over. That would be three dollars a week! I could save up my money and get Gramps something really special this Christmas. Plus, I kind of had my eye on a pair of those white go-go boots like the girls on *American Bandstand* wore. But for some reason, I didn't want to tell Gramps that's what I wanted for Christmas. I wanted him to keep thinking of me as his little tomboy. He seemed inordinately proud of the fact that I could hit a baseball as far as most of the boys on the Little League team he helped to coach.

"That's a deal." I held out my hand to shake. "And if you need any yard work done or anything like that, my friend, Jase, would be glad to help out, too." *Darn it! I wasn't going to say that. Guess I was just so happy I got carried away.*

He stood there, obviously pondering my offer. "Jase, huh?"

I nodded. I had one foot on the threshold and one on the porch.

"Would that be Jason Lee, Jed Lee's boy? The one who had that plane crash behind their house?"

"Yes." I was surprised he knew who Jase was. Everybody knew about the plane crash, of course.

"That was a sad deal, wasn't it?" He appeared to be thinking again.

"Yes, sir, it sure was. I guess it's a good thing the pilot was alone though. He wasn't married, I don't think."

"No, no. Roger wasn't married. Way I heard it was, he never got over the death of his sweetheart, Rennie Taylor."

I felt the hair on the back of my neck stand up in shock. "*The* Rennie Taylor—the woman who fell down the stairs?"

"I see you've heard of her."

"Yes. I just didn't know the pilot, Mr. Gilpin, was her sweetheart."

"Fiancée to be exact. They were supposed to be married when Roger returned from overseas. He was a Navy pilot, you see. Helped this country keep the peace in the *police-action* over in Korea back in the Fifties." There was something in the tone of his voice that told me he was being sarcastic when he said that, but I didn't know enough about the Korean War to understand what he meant. Then he continued, "But I guess he never got over it. We *all* loved Rennie. She was such a sweet girl."

"Oh, my. That's awful!" I couldn't seem to figure out exactly why this should be so important, but at the same time it seemed as if my mind was trying to tell me something that wasn't completely obvious. Sort of like when my Gramps had a problem. He always said he wanted to sleep on it 'cause his mind knew stuff that he didn't. That never made sense to me until now. It was as if my mind was trying to make a connection but my brain wouldn't let it. *Maybe when my brain goes to sleep tonight, my mind will figure it out.*

All I knew was I wanted to tell Jase about the connection between the Taylor place and Mr. Gilpin, the pilot. There was a connection there, no doubt about that. I just wasn't sure what it was yet.

As I was going out the door, I noticed another photograph tucked in behind the one of Mr. Pearcy's son and his family. This one was a black and white photo, the kind you seldom see anymore. It showed a short, stout young man scowling at the camera.

"Is that you?" I asked innocently.

Mr. Pearcy picked up the photo and held it in his hands. "That was Tom, my younger brother." He put the picture down and arranged the other one in front of it again.

I couldn't help myself. I craned my head around and took one last look at the black and white picture. Sure enough, the eyeholes appeared too deep, too dark. And the glare on the glass made it look as if the man's hair was all gone except for a few wisps clinging to the grinning white skull.

6

I jumped on my bike and hightailed it over to Billy Bob's house. I thought Jase might be there. He'd said they were going to try to get the holy water today. At least I think that's what he'd said. Actually, I was so mad and hurt that I wasn't sure what he had said. I do know I had practically hung up in his ear. I didn't want to hear what he was going to do with his best friend, Billy Bob Frank. *Who ever heard of having a first name for a last name anyhow?*

I knocked on the front door, but after a few minutes no one answered. I decided I must have missed them. I was halfway down the block headed back to my house when they swooped up on either side of me and blocked me in with their bigger bikes.

"Hey!" I yelled.

"Did we scare ya?" Billy Bob's face was pink from the sun or maybe from trying to keep up with Jase who stood about a foot taller and had legs about a mile longer.

"Sort of," I admitted. "I didn't see you coming."

Jase backed his bike up so I wasn't actually trapped. "We

were around back, pumping up my bicycle tire again. It keeps going flat."

I just nodded. "I came to tell you something I found out—"

"Look!" Billy Bob was holding up a green Coke bottle. It was half full of some liquid, but it had no lid. He had a piece of tin foil folded over the top and secured with a rubber band.

"What's that?" I had a feeling I knew, but I wasn't certain.

"Holy water!" he crowed. "We took it from my Grandma's bottle."

I swallowed. "You didn't steal it from her, did you?"

Billy Bob shook his head. "When the bottle gets toward empty, she just takes it back to the church and gets a refill. It don't cost nothin'."

Whew! Good. I didn't even take it and I felt guilty. "Okay," I said. "Now listen to this." I repeated everything Mr. Pearcy had told me.

I could see that Jase understood what I was implying, but not Billy Bob. Of course, he hadn't seen the record hit me in the face or the jelly balls falling all around us in that field. And maybe the connection wasn't *that* big. Maybe I was making too much of it. But I didn't think so. It felt huge. To find out that the ghost at Jase's house was somehow connected to the only other house in town that was supposed to be haunted too; that felt like a very big deal to me. Then there was also the fact that I kept seeing that grinning skull everywhere.

All of a sudden, a fall breeze ruffled my shirttail and I looked up at the sky and crossed my fingers behind me for good measure. I told the boys about the appearance of the skulls, and they were suitably impressed. I also remembered to tell them about the flies, holy water, and shadow men, but they didn't know what to make of that information anymore than I did. They were, however, very impressed by what I learned about Mr. Gilpin's fiancée.

"Rennie Taylor...wow." Jase's voice held the appropriate amount of awe. "Think that has anything to do with why he's still hanging around?"

"Well, it seemed important to me, but I'm just not sure why." We all started riding again at the same time.

"By the way," Jase stopped his bike again. "What'd you find out at the library about that jelly stuff? You had to go so suddenly last night I didn't get a chance to ask."

I stopped my bike beside his. I hoped my little white lie didn't show on my face. I didn't have to wash any dishes last night. Gramps and I had already done them as soon as supper was over. "Well, I looked up unusual rains and I found a few times where odd things have fallen from the sky."

"What kinds of things?" Jase asked. Billy Bob was all eyes. And ears. He'd inched his bike right up to ours without me even knowing it.

"Well, one time a bunch of rocks fell on a man's roof and caved it in."

"Rocks?" Billy Bob's voice was strident. "Huh-uh! I don't believe that." He was shaking his head back and forth like a dog with wet ears.

"Shhh!" Jase said. "Let her finish."

I glanced up at Billy Bob. "I know it sounds crazy. I'm just telling you what I read. It was in the encyclopedia. I'm not making it up, I promise." I drew an X across my heart with my pointer finger.

"What else? You said there was more."

"Another time, frogs fell, and once it was fish. Actually, the fish thing happened more than once, but in different places."

Billy Bob still looked skeptical. "How come I never heard about this stuff happening?"

"Do you read the encyclopedia?" Jase asked bluntly.

Billy had the good sense to grin and look sheepish.

At last we were on our way again, but even though we seemed to be a trio, Jase was so quiet that I began to feel excluded like before. Finally, I couldn't take it any longer. "Jason Lee!"

He jerked to a stop in front of me. His hair flopped down over his forehead and he pushed it back, planting his big feet firmly on the ground while I stared him in the eye. He looked away first, as if he knew what I was about to say.

"If you don't want me to go with y'all, tell me and I'll go home." I could hear the challenge in the tone of my voice, but I couldn't seem to stop it.

"It's not that." He pushed his hair back. "I just don't want you to get beat up again." His voice held a bit of challenge, too.

I was surprised. "I didn't get beat up. Oh, you mean jelly balls and the flying 45?"

He nodded, but didn't say anything. Billy Bob was staring at us as if we'd both lost our minds.

"Jase, I've buried my mom and my Gran, and my very best friend in the whole world moved to *California*. Jelly balls and flying records...that's nothing."

"You actually buried—" Billy's eyes were even bigger than before.

Jase rolled his eyes. "*Saw* them buried, Bill."

Billy ducked his chin and looked sheepish again. I felt bad for him. He couldn't help it if he wasn't the sharpest horn on the steer. "Sorry, Stevie."

"It's okay," I said. "I just don't want to be left out. Nothing like this has ever happened to me before. I don't understand it, but if I'm in the way just tell me."

"He was in my room again last night." Jase's voice was serious.

"What happened?" We all played statue a moment while Billy's mom and dad drove by.

"Be home before supper," Mr. Frank called out the car window.

"Okay, Dad," Billy called back. Then he waited till they were past and stuck his tongue out at his little sister who was staring at us out the back window. She did the same in return, adding the classic thumbs-in-the-ears "nana nana na na" hand wiggle to go with it. Billy Bob just grinned and gave it right back to her.

"Now," I said. "What happened?"

Jase sighed. "It's almost the same thing every time." He rubbed the hank of hair off his forehead again and swished his bike backwards and forwards for a moment, as though trying to decide how best to tell us about the ghost in his room.

I felt a cool rill of fear trickle down my spine and was not surprised to see that the sun had suddenly disappeared. I subconsciously scooted my own bike forward until all three of our front tires were barely touching. It was as if we were the only three people left in the world—at least in our little piece of it. From the corner of my eye, I saw Billy Bob squeeze his thighs together nervously, like maybe he had a sudden urge to tinkle. I couldn't help wondering what he would have done if he'd been there when the jelly balls started falling.

"So what happened?" Bill's voice sounded almost feverish. His thighs were still squeezed together across the sissy bar on his bike.

"Lady woke me up whining. She doesn't bark, just comes up and stands by my head and whines. She knows it isn't right, him being there. But I think she kind of likes the guy. He always runs his hand over her head and she quiets down."

"You mean he's that close to you? Right by your head petting Lady?" I heard a click in my throat when I swallowed. The fall leaves exuded a dry, musty odor that rode the dappled sunlight all around us.

Jase nodded slightly. "The first time, it really scared me. I pretty much screamed. You know, yelled out or something." He looked at Billy to see if his buddy would rag on him for admitting he was scared. But Billy Bob didn't say a word. He looked terrified just hearing about it. "Anyhow, that's the night I told my mom and dad." He glanced up at me to see if I remembered what they'd said.

I gave him what I hoped was an encouraging look. Of course, I remembered. I lost a lot of respect for them that day. "Then what happens, er, happened?"

Jase took a deep breath. "I always reach out to try and touch him. I mean, if he can touch Lady, then why can't I touch him?" His clear eyes were puzzled.

"But you can't?"

"No, it's just a cold misty feeling when my hand reaches the place where he should be. Like sticking your hand in the freezer, ya know? Then he always moves away. But after I reach out, he sometimes reappears at the foot of the bed or in the doorway. Once, he appeared inside my closet looking out at me. That really freaked me out. I just wanted to pull the covers over my head and forget about the whole thing."

"Oh, man!" Billy Bob was about to crush his bike with his knees. "You really see this guy every night?"

Jase blew breath out his nose. "I told you. That's why I wanted the holy water."

"Yeah, I know. But I thought you were just pullin' my leg. I didn't really *believe* you." As soon as the words were out of his mouth, he drew his head back as if expecting Jase to whack him or something. But Jase just looked at him, turned, and kicked his bike into overdrive. We had to fly to keep up.

7

In no time we were skidding to a stop in his front yard. I was out of breath and gasping. Billy was bringing up the rear. "What's the rush? Somebody light your tail on fire or something?"

"I just realized that my folks will be home soon. Our church goes longer than most, and then they usually eat lunch, but still."

We all flung our bikes down in a heap. Lady came trotting around the corner of the house to greet and shake paws. *Such a good dog.*

Jase led us to the back where Lady's self-made doggie door was pushed open. He took a stick and ran it up inside the screen and pushed up the hook that was holding the door closed. I wanted to ask why he didn't just keep a key around his neck like I did, but I figured if he wanted me to know, he'd tell me.

We'd barely got all of us inside before the fun started. Lady was standing by me, her head level with my waist, when she started to whine. I looked at Jase and he looked at me. Billy Bob was a bit slower on the uptake. He was still standing there talking when the ghost of Roger Gilpin appeared behind the kitchen table.

"So let's go look a—" Billy was saying.

"Uh, Bill?"

Billy Bob kept talking. "—round the house. You know—"

"Billy!"

"What?" he half turned and looked at me.

I motioned to the other side of the table. Billy's eyes almost popped right out of his head. His voice cut off in mid-sentence. "Oh!" he said. "I can see the wall right through him."

Lady leaned against my leg but her tail wagged slightly. She was looking directly at him. *How could he be mean if this good dog likes him?* Suddenly, I had an inspiration. "I'm not here to try and make you leave." My voice trembled. "I'm just here to try and help. We all are." I looked at Jase to see if I was doing okay. He inclined his head slightly. I felt like we were standing on eggshells, afraid to move and break the spell, afraid he would vanish as easily as he'd appeared. "Please don't throw anything at me." I smiled and wonder of wonders, the ghost smiled back. It was a sad smile though. It reminded me of Mr. Pearcy somehow.

"What can we do?" Jase's voice was surprisingly strong. "Stevie," he indicated me with his hand, "has been doing some research, and she read that maybe you need our help with something." He ended the statement with his palms turned up and open, like an invitation.

The ghost looked at me and Jase was right. His eyes *were* silver. I tried to look away, but it was hard. His eyes had no pupils. They were just like smooth silver coins shining out at me. I hoped he didn't think I was being rude, staring at him.

At last, he nodded slightly. *He did need our help.*

Okay, now we're getting somewhere, but how to find out what he needed? He didn't seem to be able to talk. I looked around the kitchen and that's when I spied it, a pile of newspapers neatly stacked and ready to become tinder for the fireplace.

"Do you have scissors?" I asked.

Jase looked at me like I'd sprung a leak—a brain leak. "You're not going to do anything violent are you? Like stab someone or something?" His voice was a whisper, but if I could hear him, then certainly Roger Gilpin could, too.

I shook my head. "Of course not. I just want to cut out letters so Mr. Gilpin can spell out words for us. He doesn't seem to be able to speak, but if he can throw records and make stuff fall from the sky, surely he can rearrange a few paper letters into words."

His eyes followed mine toward the stack of papers and understanding dawned on him in a flash. He ran to the kitchen drawer and produced two pairs of scissors. I took one and Jase ran and brought the papers to the table. "Here." He shoved a newspaper at Billy Bob. "Find us the big headlines."

In moments we had a pile of big black letters on the table. Strips of newspaper littered the kitchen floor and our hands were black with printer's ink. "Hey!"

Jase and Billy both looked up.

"Where is he?" We'd been so involved we hadn't noticed that the ghost was gone. That's when we noticed that Lady was missing, too.

Then we heard the car doors slam. In another second, the key turned in the front door. "Jase? You home?" It was his dad.

I looked down at the mess we'd made in the floor and then looked up at Mr. and Mrs. Lee standing in the doorway. "Hello," I said. They didn't know me from Adam—or Eve. I'd never met either of them.

"Hi."

Jase jumped in to save me. "This is Stevie," he said quickly. "Stevie Sanders. We're all working on a class project together."

He held up his scissors and I held up mine. I felt very transparent, as if they could see through our lie as easily as we could see through Mr. Gilpin. But Jase wasn't done. "Oh, and you already know Billy Bob." Billy just grinned. I was really hoping he wouldn't open his mouth and put our feet in, but I should have realized that of us all, Billy had the most experience at telling those little white lies. After all, he had a younger sister to blame things on.

"Don't worry," Jase rushed on. "We'll get this mess cleaned up, and anyway, Stevie has to be getting home. We'll go over there and finish it, if that's all right."

His dad was already loosening his tie, and his mother was slipping off her Sunday shoes, sliding her feet into a pair of terry cloth slippers much like the ones my own mom used to wear. Gran, too.

"That's fine, sweetie," she said. "Just—"

"Be home in time for supper. Will do." Jase found a brown paper grocery bag and started stuffing our letters inside. Billy and I scraped up all the scraps of paper from the floor and stacked them back in the pile that was now quite a bit smaller. We figured the scraps would burn just as well as the whole pages. No need to waste them.

We were almost out the back door when Jase's dad called us back.

"Yes, sir?" Jase was nothing if not polite. Still, we were worried. We thought we'd made a clean getaway. Now what?

"We ate at the church." His dad looked in the fridge while he was speaking. "Did you kids have any lunch?"

I think we actually let out a collective sigh. "Oh, yes, sir." Another lie. I was really getting worried about Jase, lying and stealing on the same day.

We hurried on outside before anyone could question us further, and as if on cue, Billy Bob's stomach let out a loud rumble. "I wish we had eaten lunch," he said glumly. "It's a long time till supper."

I laughed. "I have sandwich stuff at my house. C'mon, we'll just have to—"

Jase just stood there looking at me, waiting for my brain to catch up with my mouth.

"Oh, we can't really do this at my house." I pointed to the bag full of letters. "The ghost can't leave here."

Billy Bob groaned and slapped his forehead.

"Hey, I've got an idea."

Both boys waited.

"Why don't you tell your folks you're going to show us around? Then we can go out to the barn, and set our stuff up out there."

Jase rubbed his chin with his thumb. "We can try, I guess. I've never actually seen him out there, though."

I saw Lady coming around the corner and that's when it hit me. She was always there when the ghost was. What was it Jase had titled his story? *The Shepherd?* Maybe he had something there. "Jase."

"Yeah?"

"Why did you call your story *The Shepherd*?"

He thought about it for a moment. "'Cause when Lady was walking away with him that night, it looked like she was leading him across the field. You know, like a shepherd leading a sheep. Besides, she is a shepherd, for real."

"What are you guys talking about?" Billy Bob was looking from one of us to the other as if we had suddenly started speaking Greek.

"I wrote all this down," Jase said. "I'll show you later."

Billy nodded. "Why did you ask him about the story?" He looked at me.

"Don't you see?" Apparently, they didn't.

"Every time the ghost appears, Lady is there, too." I waited for Jase to dispute my theory. "It's like he can't go places without her. Just like you said, a shepherd leading a stray sheep."

"You may be right. I've been thinking back, and I can't remember one time when he came without her being there."

"So..."

Jase picked up on it first. "So we take Lady out to the barn and hope he shows up too. Wait right here." He stepped back inside the kitchen and we could hear him telling his folks he was going to give us the "grand tour" before we had to leave. We had to tell them something to explain why our bikes were still in a heap beside the front porch.

When he came back out, Jase said, "They were fine with that. Dad's already on the sofa in front of the ball game, Mom's lying down in her room. Dad says she's worried about my brother."

We both nodded sympathetically and headed for the barn.

"There's one other thing I don't get," he said, looking at me. "Maybe you can figure this out, too."

I waited.

"Remember in my story, I said he spoke to me at the crash site?" Jase's forehead wrinkled as he talked as if he were trying to recall every detail.

I snapped my fingers. "That's right! He did speak to you."

Jase nodded. "So why do you suppose he won't speak now? Did you find anything in your research about that?"

I chewed at my thumbnail, thinking, but I couldn't remember anything about ghosts not being able to speak. In fact, there were many cases where people could hear phantom voices in old houses. At last, I just shook my head. "Sorry," I said. "I have no idea why he can't talk anymore."

Billy Bob was listening to our conversation without comment.

"Hey!" He said suddenly, his voice excited.

We both glanced at him questioningly.

"Why don't we just ask him?"

That struck a chord on all our funny bones and we started laughing. It was funny to think it would be that simple to just ask a ghost anything.

Jase whistled for Lady, and she trotted to us without hesitation.

Inside the barn, a long worktable held various gardening tools. Jase shoved them aside and upended the paper bag so that our heaps of letters fell out. We all looked around to see if the ghost had followed Lady.

At first, no one saw anything unusual. But while we were all looking elsewhere, a few of the letters started to whirl gently about as though a slight breeze had sprung up just above the table.

We all stared wide-eyed as the crudely scissored letters began to line up like words. I wanted to look around, especially behind me, but I wouldn't let myself. I had to see what was taking shape on the table.

First, an R floated down, then an E and two Ns. When those were followed by the letters I and E, I knew we were on to something. I allowed my gaze to wander, and sure enough, there in the far corner stood Lady. Roger Gilpin was beside her with his hand stroking her head. His other hand was making little swirly motions in the air. The motions exactly matched the motions of the letters falling silently onto the tabletop.

The boys saw where I was looking, and then they saw him, too. This time, his silver eyes were closed, as if he were concentrating. That made it a lot easier to look at him, or rather, through him. We could actually see the outline of the wooden ladder that led up to the haymow.

As if we were one person, the three of us looked back at the table. The words RENNIE OT HERE were spelled out there. We all gazed at each other in confusion. OT. What was that word? Did he mean to write TO and just got it mixed up?

Then Jase whispered, "Look." He pointed to the place between the first and second words. There was an extra space there, like a blank.

Quickly I shuffled through the remaining letters. There were no more Ns. None at all. He'd used the only two Ns to spell out RENNIE.

"Rennie NOT here," Billy Bob breathed. "Not where? Here in the barn?"

I shook my head. "I think he's saying she's not where he is...over there."

Both boys nodded their agreement. That's the only thing that made sense.

"But if she died, too, why wouldn't she be wherever he is?" Jase asked.

"Well, remember that one book said if a person died violently their spirit might remained trapped."

"Oh." Jase and Billy looked at each other. "Maybe that's why they say the old Taylor place is haunted. Maybe Rennie Taylor's spirit is trapped there."

Billy Bob yanked out his inhaler and took a deep puff. I recalled what Jase had told me about Billy never getting past the front porch at the Taylor place.

I was chewing the cuticle around my thumbnail. The boys were congratulating each other on the connection they'd made. "There's just one thing though."

They looked at me none too kindly. They did not want me to burst their bubble, but I had to say it. "Rennie Taylor just fell down the stairs. Why would that trap her spirit? I mean that's an accident, not a violent death. Just very sad that she was so young." I was congratulating myself on making my *own* connections when suddenly a roaring gust of wind whipped through the open door and all the letters on the table flew up to the ceiling in the shape of a twisting, swirling whirlwind—what some people call a dust-devil.

"Make it stop!"

I think that was Billy, but I'm not sure. It could have been me. Straw and dirt and other debris from the barn floor swirled around with the letters and we all ducked and covered our eyes.

When we opened them, two new words were spelled out on the table. NO ACCIDENT.

We glanced at the corner where the pilot ghost, Mr. Roger Gilpin, was staring at us with his shiny silver eyes.

"So she must be trapped there." I was so excited. "Is that right?" I was directing my question at the ghost. He nodded—at least I think he did. And I jumped up and down as if I'd just won the relay race in PE. "Now we know what's going on," I said happily. I couldn't understand why the guys weren't elated, too. Finally I stopped hopping and jumping. "What?" I looked at Jase. "Aren't you happy to know why you have a ghost haunting your room?"

"Yep," his voice didn't sound happy. "That's great."

I looked at the corner where the ghost was still stroking Lady's head.

"But now," Jase continued. "What do we do about it?"

I sat down on a rough wooden sawhorse bench. "Well, we just, I mean we need to..." I looked up at him helplessly. "Holy water?"

The letters began to twitch again. The ghost wanted our attention. But he didn't change the words. They just twitched around and then resettled exactly as they had been. NO ACCIDENT.

"What does it mean if she fell down the stairs but it wasn't an accident?" As soon as the words were out of my mouth, I knew. We all did.

New letters rearranged themselves to just one more word: PUSHED.

"Do you know who did it?" I asked. I looked at the corner, but Mr. Gilpin had gone so pale and transparent that I couldn't see if he was shaking his head no, or nodding it for yes.

Finally, the letters whirled and shivered, then settled back down. All that was left on the table was the word NO.

"So, if you don't know who did it, how do you know it wasn't an accident?" I couldn't believe I was standing there talking to a ghost.

The letters began to spin all around the cozy barn again. But this time it seemed they would never stop, and it wasn't just a breeze or a small whirlwind. This time it was a miniature tornado. We dove under the table and waited for the storm to pass. I saw a trowel go spinning across the barn and dig its tines into a bale of hay in the loft. In quick succession, the other gardening tools flew upward and stuck into various positions in the hay also.

I was on my knees praying that those were the only sharp things on the table when, as suddenly as it began, it was over. Things settled back down and we came crawling out. I was mad. Throwing records and blobs of jelly was one thing, but slinging sharp tools around was another. We could've been killed.

In the middle of the table were these words: SORRY REN NOT HERE COS MURDER.

We all looked at the corner where he'd been standing, but the ghost pilot was gone. And so was Lady.

8

We dashed out to the field and sure enough, Lady was standing with her back to us looking away toward the horizon. It was midafternoon now, and we were all starving. "C'mon," I said. "Let's go get something to eat, then I can make up an excuse to go see Mr. Pearcy and question him some more."

Together, we cleaned up the barn, but we didn't discard the letters. We tucked them safely back into the paper bag and stored it beneath the worktable. Jase and Billy climbed the ladder to the loft, what Jase called the haymow, and retrieved the gardening tools. "Why don't we store those in a better place, if that's okay?" I didn't want them flying around our heads if we had to use the barn with Mr. Gilpin again.

At last we jumped on our bikes and headed to my house. I thought it was strange that Jase didn't even feel the need to go in and say goodbye to his folks. "They're busy," he said. "They hardly know I'm around anymore. But that's all right. They're just too worried about my brother to think of anything else except church where they go to pray for him all the time."

We rode in near silence for a while with Lady loping along

beside us, doing her best to stay in the shade of the overhanging oaks.

"We forgot to ask him why he couldn't speak!" Billy sounded disappointed.

Jase and I groaned in unison. "We didn't really have a chance," Jase said. "But I have a theory."

We all slowed in order to hear.

"Did you guys notice how he closed his eyes to make the letters move?"

We nodded.

"And did you see how he got more and more transparent the longer he was with us?"

"Yeah! You're right, he did." I had noticed, but I hadn't thought anything of it until now. "So you think maybe he's getting weaker or something? Like he only has so long before he has to move on?"

"That's all I can think of," he replied. "But it's just a theory. When I saw him at the crash site, he looked like a real man, but his voice was strange, like his eyes. Flat, you know?"

I did know. Those eyes were the spookiest thing about him, except for his transparency and the fact that he would just show up without warning.

"Still got your holy water?" I asked Billy.

He lifted the edge of his shirt and showed me how he had it tucked into the waistband of his jeans. I couldn't believe it had been there this whole time. "A bit might have spilled out in the barn," he said. "But I think my jeans soaked it up."

Jase and I exchanged looks of awe. But we didn't say anything. The episode in the barn was so *real*. It was even more impressive than getting hit with a record and jelly rain. A woman had died, and it was beginning to look like she'd actually been murdered. But who did it? Who would have wanted to kill the woman Mr. Gilpin wanted to marry?

My Gramps was picking the tomatoes from his fall garden when we arrived.

"We'll have pumpkins soon," he said. "Just in time for Halloween."

The boys were suitably impressed. Gramps handed us each a warm, sun-ripened cherry tomato and we ate it right there in the garden. It was delicious. But the tiny red fruit only whetted our appetites and made us hungry for more, so we hurried to the kitchen and made lettuce, cheese, and tomato sandwiches. We'd finished off the bologna the day before. We washed it all down with ice cold water from the big glass jug we kept filled in the fridge.

"What now?" Gramps asked when we'd eaten him out of house and home.

"Going to the park," I said. Again, I crossed my fingers behind my back and made myself another mental note to actually go to the park after we left Mr. Pearcy's house. That way I wouldn't really be lying, just not telling all the truth.

We were lucky. Mr. Pearcy was on his front porch when we rode by. That gave us an excuse to stop for a visit.

I introduced Billy Bob and then Jase. "Remember? We were talking about Jase just this morning. He's the one who had the plane crash in his back yard."

Mr. Pearcy nodded. "Tragedy," he said. "I heard the doc say he thought Roger had just run low on fuel and tried to land in your back field."

"That's what my dad heard, too. Said if it hadn't been blowing so hard, he might have made it." Jase shook his head as if to clear away the still-fresh memory.

"Two tragedies," Mr. Pearcy said. It was like he was almost speaking to himself, or thinking out loud. "First his girl, then him. Seems like trouble just follows some folks."

"Had they always been sweethearts?" I tried to sound nonchalant, but my heart was pounding in my chest.

"Oh, no. Well, almost. There was another who thought she was sweet on him, but you know I told you Rennie was nice to everyone. This boy insisted on hanging around, even after she'd made it known she was engaged to Roger. But like I said, Rennie was just so kind. She even tried to be friends with the other boy. Let him down easy, you know." He stopped and looked at us as if surprised we were there. "We were all in the same class," he admitted. "Guess I'll never get over the way her death affected everyone. Back in school, Roger and Rennie were golden. Seemed to have everything, those two."

I jumped in while I had the chance. "Who was the other boy? Is he still around?"

Mr. Pearcy stood and shuffled across the porch, preparing to go back inside the house. For a moment, I thought he wasn't going to answer, thought we must've tired him out or something. Then he said, "He was my brother." He must have seen how confused I looked, because he added, "You know, my younger brother." An expression of such utter sadness crossed his face that I felt myself gasp. But he had turned and slipped through the screen door before any of us could react.

For a moment, the three of us were frozen in silence. Then we scurried to our bikes and without a word, headed straight for the old Taylor place. No one hesitated when we got to the gate, although Jase made sure he held it tightly while we all rode through. Right up on the porch we went, except for Billy Bob.

I pushed open the screeching door and stepped inside. The air was just as gloomy and dusty as before, the light just as dim. Jase was right beside me. I could hear him breathing. Lady was there too, trembling in between Jase and me. I was about to ask him what we should do next when the door slammed shut behind us.

We turned just in time to catch a glimpse of Bill's shocked face at the bottom of the porch steps. His mouth was open in a perfect O of surprise.

"Now what?" I whispered. Lady pressed against my leg, then headed for the stairs. In a moment, she was at the top.

"I'm going up," Jase said.

I grabbed the tail of his shirt. "You're not leaving me here alone."

The stairs were dark. Every step made some sort of noise, as if protesting us being there.

"Jase!" I gasped and pointed to the wall. The short, stout, shadow of a man was creeping along the hallway toward us.

"In here." Jase pulled me into an empty room and we quickly closed the door. I said a silent prayer of thanks when the door didn't screech or squeak like the one downstairs. Maybe we'd be safe in here. I huddled beside Jase, wondering where Lady had gone.

"Who was that?" I whispered.

Jase shrugged and opened his mouth to speak when something banged the door right beside our heads.

We jumped and scrambled across the room looking for another exit or even a closet to hide in, but it was an old house, and closets were not built-in back then.

I was just about to try to pry open the window when we heard a volley of barking. Lady was going nuts down the hallway. Jase rushed to the door and yanked it open. The hall was empty except for Lady. She was standing near a room on the other side of the staircase. She was so excited and upset we could see drops of saliva fly from her mouth each time she barked.

Jase nudged me and pointed to the room opposite the landing. Craning our necks, we could barely see into the room. Weak sunlight struggled through the window and cast shadows there, but this time, the man's shadow wasn't alone. It was joined by the delicate shape of a woman wearing an old-fashioned dress, the kind that came down below the knees like those the girls wore back in the nineteen fifties. "Are they really in there?"

Jase nodded. Lady was still barking like crazy. Then she disappeared into the room and we heard her toenails clattering across the floorboards. Suddenly the spirits were there—right in front of us—and they were scuffling. If I strained my ears I thought I could hear angry words, but that couldn't be right. Ghosts didn't talk. Mr. Gilpin didn't anyway. But maybe these were different. The stout shape certainly *looked* evil. He appeared to be menacing the slender woman. He had hold of her arms, as if he was trying to force her to look at him.

Jase lunged toward them.

"Wait," I cried. "They're only spirits." But it was too late. The lady—Rennie Taylor—broke free and turned to run.

Desperately, the shadow man grabbed at her, but instead of grasping her, he knocked her off balance and she tumbled down the staircase with a sickening series of thuds, and bumps, and thumps. Then all was silent.

That wasn't right. Spirits shouldn't make noise falling down stairs. Maybe the shadow man had fallen, too. I knew *he* could make noise. No doubt he was the one who had frightened us by pounding on the bedroom door. But where was he now? Even Lady had stopped barking. And where was Jase?

I dashed to the head of the stairs and peered over the railing. The ghost of the woman lay crumpled at the bottom of the stairs and the dark shape of the man was kneeling over her, but there was another shape there, too. A solid, blond-haired boy crouched on the bottom stair holding his shoulder and watching the sad tableau unfolding before him.

Sure enough, something about the stout man's head reminded me of Mr. Pearcy and, at the same time, it reminded me of that grinning skull. I knew at any moment the angry ghost was going to turn his head and look up at me with those black, empty eyes.

Then out of the gloom came the tinkling echo of breaking glass followed by a whistling sound, and the green Coke bottle holding the holy water landed right in the midst of the shadow-couple with a crash. Water splashed the spirits and puddled darkly on the bare wood floor. Thin tendrils of smoke drifted up. Both shadowy shapes dissolved and disappeared.

Lady dashed down the stairs with me right on her heels. Jase was standing, holding on to the railing with one hand. I could see Billy Bob's face pressed to what remained of the glass in the multi-paned front window. "The door wouldn't open," he yelled.

I ran over and pulled. It opened easily. Billy strode inside. "I swear I tried. It wouldn't open!"

"It's okay," I said. "You did great—perfect timing. I think the ghosts are gone."

"It wasn't me," Billy said. Then he stepped aside and I could see Mr. Pearcy standing behind him.

"I saw you all go through the gate." His face was grim. "I couldn't take a chance on my brother hurting someone else."

Jase glanced around slowly. "Where's Lady?"

We all looked about and Jase called, but she didn't reappear. We hurried outside. She wasn't in the front yard. The three of us dashed around the corner of the house just in time to see Lady leading two shapes toward the setting sun. One shape was tall, with a shock of silvery hair. The other was smaller, and slim, wearing an old fashioned dress that fell to just below her knees.

None of us said a word. We didn't know what to say.

"What did you kids think you were doing here?" Mr. Pearcy asked. He'd followed us around the corner at a much slower pace. I wasn't sure if he'd seen the retreating shapes or not.

"We were just looking for my dog," Jase said innocently.

"I *thought* I heard barking, but I knew there hadn't been a dog here since Roger took back Rennie's shepherd pup all those years ago after she died." Mr. Pearcy shook his head as if he'd had enough memories for one day. "He had just given her that pup for her birthday before he went to Korea. Guess he felt like Lady belonged to him as much as she did to Rennie. As soon as his tour of duty was up, he came home and Rennie's mom gave Lady back to him. 'Course she was about a year old by then."

The three of us looked at each other. "Rennie Taylor had a German shepherd named Lady?"

"Oh, yes," he replied. "They were inseparable. You know that dog disappeared ten years to the day after Rennie fell down those stairs." He clicked his tongue against his teeth in disbelief. "Roger told me it was like losing his sweetheart all over again. Never found hide nor hair of her either."

I gulped.

Jase did, too. "My dog is named Lady," he said. "I found her ten years ago today. She'd been hit by a car and left for dead." He looked up at Mr. Pearcy. The older man was nodding thoughtfully.

The air was thick with thoughts of possibility. Billy Bob was standing quietly. He appeared to be mulling something over in his mind. "Uh, sir?"

"Yes?"

We were slowly walking back toward the front of the house. I glanced toward the field, but there was nothing behind us now except for the yellow, orange, and pink streaks of the sunset.

"Why did you throw the holy water?" Billy Bob asked. "Did you see Miss Rennie and—and that other shape?" He tried to make his voice as soft as possible.

"Of course I didn't see anything." Mr. Pearcy's eyes were flinty. "But the door was locked. We had to use something to break the window, didn't we?"

We all looked at each other. Hadn't he said he didn't want his brother to hurt anyone else?

"Yes, yes, I know what you're thinking." Mr. Pearcy sighed. "I suspected he was still here somehow. He was the boy who followed her around all the time. We always lived just down the street. Everybody knew he was sweet on her. He never made any secret of it. Always showing up at the house, unannounced. Just couldn't seem to accept it when she got engaged to Roger."

"Sounds like that girl, Joanie," Billy Bob whispered loudly to Jase. "The one who stole your ID bracelet."

Jase scowled at him.

The older man got that wistful look again. "You know, my brother took his own life after Rennie died. He drove his car right into their garage here and well, I think he was just devastated with guilt." He seemed to remember that he was talking to a bunch of kids because he cut off his own sentence and turned on his heel. "That's the other reason I threw Billy's Coke bottle." His eyes were mild, but his voice shook. "Whatever I saw in there. I hope it's gone now."

We all shrugged. "I didn't really see what happened," I said, as I crossed my fingers behind my back. "It was just a bunch of shadows." I thought one more white lie wasn't too bad considering what we'd accomplished today.

Jase sat down on the porch step and Mr. Pearcy examined his shoulder. "Nothing broken, thank God, just very bruised. It was a miracle if you ask me."

9

Several days later, over Cokes at Dal Paso Drug Store, the three of us argued about whether we really had released the spirits of Roger Gilpin and Rennie Taylor. Jase said we had. He hadn't been visited anymore, and Lady hadn't returned, either. But none of us were sure about Tom, Mr. Pearcy's brother. We hadn't seen him walking away. Billy said he thought the guy's spirit might still be in the garage at the old house. I guess it's possible. That's one thing I just don't want to know.

One thing I am sure of, Lady must've been the key. It was a turning point, I suppose. When Mr. Gilpin's plane crashed in Jase's yard, it was what she'd been waiting for. It was like her job to get Roger and Rennie back together. Was Lady a ghost, too? I haven't figured that one out yet. Neither has Jase, although we've talked about it many times.

The whole thing was a turning point for me, too. Karla never moved back, but we continued to write letters back and forth, and after a few more months, I didn't miss her quite as much. Me and Jase and Billy Bob, we became sort of inseparable. Billy called us the Three Mouseketeers. I thought it was kind of silly, but in a good way. No, make that, in a *great* way.

I went ahead and went to work for Mr. Pearcy, and Jase did, too. But there's one thing few people know about my time spent there. The first thing I did every time I walked in the front door was to turn that old black and white photo on the table toward the wall. I know it seems impossible, but every once in awhile, I swear it looked like a grinning skull was staring out at me.

And you know what? That wasn't the only strange thing I saw when I was young.

It seemed like Jase and Lady and Mr. Gilpin opened up a whole new world of otherness for me. The next year, after we'd solved the riddle of Rennie Taylor's death, I had to enlist Jase's aid on another ghostly problem. This time, I was the one being haunted. But that's another tale for another time.

ABOUT THE AUTHOR

Ann is the author of numerous published short stories. This is her first novella.

Also Read:

Book Two: Stevie-girl and The Phantom Student

Book Three: Stevie-girl and The Phantom of Crybaby Bridge.

Continue reading for an excerpt from book two in the Phantom series, *Stevie-girl and the Phantom Student*.

For more information

www.annswann.blogspot.com

Stevie-girl and the Phantom Student
Ann Swann
Book Two of the Phantom Series

STEVIE-GIRL AND THE PHANTOM
STUDENT

To us, 1970 was a time of beginnings, but to the country, it was a time of endings. National Guardsmen ended the lives of four students at Kent State College. A hundred thousand marched on Washington to end the war in Vietnam, and in England, Paul McCartney announced the end of The Beatles. It was also the year Jimi Hendrix and Janis Joplin both ended their lives through drug overdoses. It felt as if the whole world was in turmoil.

Our homeroom teacher said not to let the weight of the world stop us from being open to new experiences. In fact she said it was more important than ever that we should be open-minded. I wondered if she'd gone radical on us. For a moment, I thought she might pick up a sign and start chanting.

Come to find out, she was simply prepping us for a new addition to our eighth grade class at Crossroads Junior High. His name was Derol Pavey and he had something called Tourette syndrome.

STEVIE-GIRL AND THE PHANTOM
STUDENT ~ CHAPTER ONE

"**W**hat's up?" Jase's voice was low, but then he was never very loud. Guess that's why we got along so well.

I smiled up at him. "Not much." I shifted my books from the crook of one arm to the crook of the other. "What's up with you?"

Jase grimaced. I could tell he wanted to say something.

I elbowed him in the ribs as we made our way across home-room to our desks in the back corner. "Why are you making that face? What's wrong?"

"Nothing really," he replied, his usually clear green eyes clouded and mysterious. "It's just that, well. Have you heard about Janis Joplin?"

That got my attention. I loved Janis Joplin. Jase acciden-tally caught me wailing away to one of her records one after-noon when I was supposed to meet him in front of my house. When I wasn't outside, he just opened the screen door and came on inside. He said he could hear my yowling as soon as his feet cleared the threshold. After that, I always locked the front door before singing my Janis tunes.

"What about her?" I asked, a pang of unease settling in my stomach like the cherry pit I'd accidentally swallowed when I was about five. Jimi Hendrix, who had electrified Woodstock only thirteen months earlier, had overdosed on a combination of drugs and alcohol just a couple of weeks earlier. And everyone knew Janis was every bit as wild as Jimi. Maybe even wilder.

Jase looked up as several other students entered the class-room. "They found her in a motel room yesterday. She overdosed."

I looked at the psychedelic pink and purple swirls deco-rating my notebook. Snippets of my favorite Janis song, *Piece of My Heart,* swirled through my head in patterns that seemed very similar.

"Oh." My voice was small. I couldn't seem to say anything else. Janis was a big star. She wasn't a friend or an acquaintance, but she *was* young and famous. She shouldn't have died. She and Hendrix were both only twenty-seven years old. I hated when people just up and died without warning. It happened all the time in my little corner of the world. Even though I had already lost both my Mom and my Gran, I guess I thought famous people should be immune to death or something. Irra-tional tears started in the corners of my eyes and began a lazy trek toward my chin.

Jase reached across the aisle between our desks. His hand was large and firm when he grasped my shoulder. I'd taken hold of that hand on more than one occasion when he had to help me across a ditch or even the time I had to help him up after he fell down the stairs in the old haunted Taylor mansion. But this show of concern right in front of everyone in the class, this was something altogether different.

I shrugged my shoulder so he would take his hand away.

He didn't get mad or upset. Jase didn't get mad. He understood me pretty well. He knew I didn't like to be the center of attention. I smiled at him to let him know I appreciated the gesture of friendship, but I felt silly sitting there crying over someone who had caused her own demise by doing things that were illegal and stupid.

Somehow, I'd identified with Janis, that's why I'd admired her. She succeeded even though she was different—maybe because she was different. It was as if she had taken her outcast image and made it larger than life. I could never do that, even if I did feel the same way. But I could relate to her, and I could admire her for it, and now she was gone, so I guess now I could grieve for her, too.

I might have sat there wallowing in grief for the whole twenty-minute class period except that Derol Pavey chose that moment to make his entrance.

When he stepped through the door and stood hesitantly in front of the class waiting for Mrs. Flint to acknowledge him, the excitement in the room was as thick as cream, but not nearly as sweet. In fact, there was a sour feeling, as if every student had just run a dozen laps at P.E. and then skipped the showers.

Mrs. Flint took a deep breath. She'd tried to prepare us, but maybe that was part of the problem. We could sense her uncertainty and it transferred to us as if by electrical current. "Class," she said. "This is Derol Pavey. He is the new student I told you about from The Philippines."

Ahhh, so that explained it. Not only did the kid suffer from something called Tourette syndrome, he also suffered the dreaded curse of being from "somewhere else." His skin was a dusky bronze color and his night-black hair was shiny and razor-straight.

He peered at us from eyes almost as black as his hair and then the oddest thing happened. His left arm flew up and he barked like a hoarse dog. *Rarf. Rarf.*

Mrs. Flint grabbed his arm as if to hold it in place, but that only made his other arm fly up. His notebook hit the floor and popped open scattering loose-leaf paper everywhere.

Susan Jansen and Juanita Silva were in their customary front row seats. They immediately jumped up and began to gather the paper. They attempted to stuff it back into the sprung clasps of the blue canvas-covered notebook, but Derol, still barking, suddenly began to pirouette like a stout canine ballerina. Mrs. Flint was dragged around in a circle a time or two before she got wise and turned loose of his arm, but it was too late. The class was in tatters, some giggled, others gasped in shock, and some of us simply sat in stunned and silent disbelief.

Then as if summoned by magic, Mr. Terrance, the assistant principal, arrived and took hold of poor Derol and ushered him, still twirling and waving his arms, from the room. We could hear them out in the hall, Derol barking and Mr. Terrance shushing.

Janis was forgotten. Jimi was forgotten. My sadness was forgotten. Mrs. Flint flopped down heavily in her tri-wheeled teacher's chair and mopped at her forehead with a crumpled Kleenex from her sweater pocket.

"That didn't go as planned," she muttered. Then she seemed to remember where she was so she leapt to her feet and clapped her hands together smartly. "Class!" she said. "Come to order." She motioned toward Juanita and Sally who were still clutching handfuls of paper. "Girls, bring me all that and let's try and get back on track."

The two girls hurried to the front of the room and turned over their treasure.

"Now," the teacher continued. "I must apologize. I'm certain I could've handled that better. Poor Derol. I'm afraid I made things worse. He really can't help himself. We must all remember that." She patted at her short, fluffy hair. It was obvious to all of us that she had no idea how things had gotten so squirrely so quickly.

"Going to be an interesting year," Jase whispered with a wicked grin.

I couldn't help it, I laughed in spite of myself.